Praise for NEVE

"An intense psychological study of obsession, ~~~~~ ~
hubris, set on the body-strewn slopes of Everest - with a deft
hand on the mountain's unearthly and supernatural elements
- T.L. Bodine's novel gripped me throughout. Perfect for
fans of Amy McCulloch's *Breathless*, or Sarah Lotz's *The
White Road*."
— Ally Wilkes, author of *All the White Spaces*

"NEVEREST weaves a deft, intoxicating spell of grief, in-
trigue, adventure, and the ghosts of our pasts. Beautifully
paced and haunting in all the best ways, by the end of the
journey I felt almost as breathless as a doomed climber.
Bodine spins a talented and imminently enjoyable tale—settle in for winter horror at its best."
— Laurel Hightower, author of *Crossroads* and *Below*

"With an uncanny ability to bring the most brutal emotions
out of her characters, Bodine's writing will suck you in as
you claw to the top of the mountain with them, the low
thrum of dread pulsing with every step."
— Donna Taylor, author of the *San Nico Slayers* series

"An emotional slow-burn facing the power of the elements.
From the start, *Neverest* is harsh, thoughtful, and real to its
core. I felt the cold of this book snapping at my bones."
— Hailey Piper, Bram Stoker Award-winning author of
Queen of Teeth

"T.L. Bodine's *Neverest* is a beautifully written exploration
of the ascent to Everest and what it means to retrace the
steps of a lost life. The novel climbs to a truly expansive and
stunning peak."
—Christi Nogle, Bram Stoker Award® nominated author of
Beulah

NEVEREST
T.L BODINE

Neverest

ISBN (paperback): 978-1-7396116-4-4

ISBN (e-book): 978-1-7396116-5-1

Cover illustration © Donnie Kirchner

Book formatting and cover design by Claire Saag

For David,

who's helped me climb my own sort of mountain.

CHAPTER ONE

The plane trembles on its descent, and Carrie wonders whether it might crash.

Through her fogged-over porthole window, she can see the rapidly approaching slope. Trees grow impossibly large as the tiny plane sweeps over and past them. She glimpses the place where the tree line stops further up the mountain range, that bleak border between arable land and bitter, windswept rock. But then the plane jolts, swoops downward, and the peaks disappear from view. The sky is gone, too. Only forest is visible, evergreens looming around and above, as if the plane has entered a bowl turned on its side.

The plane ceases its downward trajectory, slowing as it approaches the airport laterally. Landing will be an issue not so much of coming to ground, but of meeting the improbably placed landing strip head-on.

The airport itself, if 'airport' is even the right word for something so small and precariously placed, seems to be nothing more than a narrow patch of dark pavement cutting through a carved-out space in the mountain. It ends abruptly at the edge of a cliff, making take-off a do-or-die scenario. Every departure would have to be an act of faith that the plane had built up enough speed to stay airborne once it reached that sudden drop-off.

Carrie shifts in her seat, one hand against the window, and cranes her neck for a better look at the cliff face below. Scanning for a glimpse of metal, the mangled corpses of air-planes that failed to launch or came in to land at the wrong angle. But she can make out nothing but trees and that as-phalt runway looming ever larger in her view. The scenery whips past at nauseating speed.

The plane is tiny, seating less than twenty passengers— one on each side of the narrow center aisle. Unlike the in-ternational jet that brought her to Kathmandu, this plane was not built for comfort or luxury. It exists only to shuttle pas-sengers from the city up to the Tenzing-Hillary Airport, and its only job is to land without killing everyone aboard. Car-rie can only hope it manages to do that job.

She turns away from the window and leans back against the headrest of her seat, squeezing her eyes shut as they swoop in for the final approach. Her fingers curl over the edge of the armrest, nails biting into the thin fabric.

It's strange not to feel Sean's hand there, not to lace her fingers through his.

He had never liked to fly. She'd always made fun of him for it. Sean Miller, outdoorsman, mountaineer, explorer— afraid of airplanes. She teased him for it when they honeymooned in Japan. It felt comforting, somehow, that the man she married, the man who made a career of being in danger, still had some things that frightened him.

"It's a control thing," he'd explained, almost sulking. "On the mountain, I can set the ropes, I can catch myself if I start to fall. I at least have a fighting chance. But if the plane goes down, what am I supposed to do about it?"

"Fatal plane crashes are less than one in a million," she reminded him.

But that was at a normal airport, on a normal airplane. The odds weren't as promising here. Tenzing-Hillary had the dubious honor of being the world's deadliest airport, where high-profile crashes happened every few years. She'd made the mistake of reading about them when she booked the trip. She hadn't meant to, but it was difficult to search 'flights from Chicago to Mount Everest' without seeing headlines about the airport in Lukla and the multiple crashes there over the last decade alone. Once she read one, she was compelled to read the rest, becoming something of a five-minute expert on the topic—one of many things to fill her brain since first planning this trip. Thanks to her reading, she knows that the airport's short runway with its mountain backdrop hardly makes for a forgiving landing space. There is no cushion to compensate for landing gear failure or a plane that veers off course. If a plane comes in too fast, or at the wrong angle, or without its landing gear in good working order, nothing will stop it from over-shooting and careening right into the mountain.

None of this knowledge brings her comfort.

Carrie keeps her eyes squeezed shut.

She feels a jolt, a heavy thump, and her heart leaps into her throat before she realizes it's the landing gear hitting pavement. Hard deceleration drives her back hard into her seat. She thinks she might be sick. She's not normally prone to motion sickness, but the combination of altitude and nerves have turned her guts to a tangled, watery mess.

She swallows back bile and grits her teeth against the impulse to vomit.

It takes her a moment to realize that the plane has stopped. Her eyes squeezed tightly shut, jaws aching from the way she's pressed her teeth together, she still feels the phantom sensation of movement. Her surroundings spin and dip around her like she's had a night of heavy drinking. One hand has left its death-grip on the arm rest and found the chain at her throat instead.

Sean had always worn his ring on a chain rather than his finger, explaining that the cold and altitude could shrink or swell the flesh, making it easier to lose the ring or get hurt if it cut into the skin. She decided to follow his advice, threading her matching ring onto a chain before boarding the connecting flight from Chicago to New York. She clings to that wedding band now like a talisman, the way someone might grasp a rosary, and the cool weight of the platinum against her skin has a soothing effect.

Slowly, the world stops spinning. Carrie dares to open her eyes.

Other passengers rise from their seats, squeezing together in the claustrophobic center aisle, a crush of bodies moving toward the door. She stays in her seat and waits for the crowd to clear, waits for the nausea to pass. If she's going to vomit, she wants to do it without an audience.

Two months from now, when the expedition is over, she'll have to come back to this airport and climb into this plane or another like it. She'll have to feel the world drop away as she's launched slingshot-style out of the mountains. The idea of willingly enduring that seems preposterous. She's only just arrived and she's already dreading her impending departure.

Did Sean feel the same way, she wonders?

Did he worry then about the flight home? Or did he know, somehow, that he would never fly again?

"It's not what he would have wanted."

Tom was firm on that point. He had repeated it several times already, with increasing intensity. At first, it had been quiet, almost plaintive, like a suggestion meant to be sub-liminal. The way you nudge someone into recognizing some obvious and embarrassing thing about themselves, allowing them to save face. But, several rounds of drinks later, the discussion had begun to spiral, a recursive orbit that always came back to the same points. Each time it came up, he grew more emphatic. He sounded almost angry now. Accusatory, like she was being selfish or stubborn on purpose just to piss him off.

"You don't know what he'd have wanted," Carrie told him, the intensity of her rebuttal matching his. "You weren't even there for him! Nobody was there!"

If Tom could throw out accusations, she could, too.

The grief was a fresh, bleeding wound.

The memorial had ended hours ago. Mourners had come and gone, lingering to give hugs and casseroles and platitudes. Most of her family were there, although none of them looked like they wanted to be. Only a few relatives of Sean's were there. The rest were scattered to the wind. She'd never met most of his family, and now she would never have an occasion to change that. There were a ton of mountain-climbing friends, though. An entire mountaineering association's worth of climbers had come to pay their respects, huddled together to talk among themselves and ignore the curious looks from people who wondered at their sunburnt faces and intermittently missing fingers, noses, limbs. At least they'd mostly had the courtesy to shave, although there were one or two shaggy mountain men among them.

Most of the climbers left for the bar after the service was over. Carrie had stayed home to throw her own sort of after-party, if that was the right word for the hard drinking that came on the night of a funeral. She'd never been clear on the rules and customs surrounding all of that. She hadn't even planned the service. She'd left it up to her mother and a cluster of aunts, the sort of busy-fingered, gossiping Midwestern women whose talents ran in precisely that direction. The same group of women who had resented Carrie's refusal to let them help plan the wedding. Ironic, really, that they should get their chance at a big event now.

Regardless, Carrie had gone home and uncorked a bottle of wine and cried, and dear friends had comforted her as best they could before finding some reason they could no longer stay, and she'd opened up a second bottle when the first ran dry.

Now it was just her and Tom. They sat in the kitchen that Sean had never finished remodeling—a project he'd never quite found time for—beer bottles piling up in front of him, wine corks in front of her. The ceiling fan wobbled overhead, the light flickering slightly as it trembled. Outside, it had gone from evening to night to the earliest hours of morning, time stubbornly refusing to stand still for grief. Darkness concealed the world beyond the patio door.

"It hurts, Carrie. It fucking hurts. I get that. You don't have to tell me." He leaned back, holding his beer by the neck. "But it won't change anything."

His light brown eyes were bloodshot, his hair even more disheveled than usual. It looked like he hadn't slept in days, and truthfully, he probably hadn't. He'd taken the red-eye to Chicago as soon as he'd heard. He hadn't even waited for her to call. The news went out over the expedition website, and he was on the plane within hours. He'd barely thought to pack a change of clothes. He'd had to buy a tie for the memorial—insisted on it, even though Carrie had told him it didn't fucking matter, that nobody cared what he was wearing—and had worn the same dress shoes he'd worn at their wedding seven years earlier because they were the only dress shoes he owned.

He was here, now. He was the first to arrive and had stayed even after everyone had gone. But it wasn't enough. Because he hadn't been there then, when it could have made a difference.

That knowledge settled between them, a wedge driven deep.

It wasn't fair to blame Tom for what had happened on the mountain, but Carrie needed to cast a villain.

"It's just so senseless." She looked down at her empty wine glass, rolling the stem between her fingers. "It doesn't even feel real. I don't think it will ever feel real until I see him."

Her eyes ached, but she couldn't cry anymore. She wasn't sure she'd ever be able to cry again. She felt utterly spent and knew she'd have the worst hangover of her life in the morning and couldn't find it in herself to care.

Tom dropped his gaze, silent for a long time. When he spoke at last, he sounded sober. The harsh, flat gleam of liquor seemed absent from his eyes as they rolled upward, seeking hers. "Give it time," he said, and, before she could interrupt, "If you change your mind—if this is still what you want a year from now—then I'll go with you. I'll take you there, and we'll look together. I promise."

He didn't mean to keep the promise. Carrie suspected it at the time and grew sure as the months passed. He'd just said it in order to placate her. He thought once she was sober, once the grief had lost its edge, once time had an opportunity to intervene, that she'd change her mind.

He didn't intend to keep the promise, but he wouldn't go back on it once it had been made.

Tom Fisher was the kind of guy who would spend the last of his money on a cross-country red-eye to his best friend's memorial service. He was the kind of guy who kept his word, even if the terms were impossible or insane.

Carrie knew it. She almost felt guilty, holding him to his offer. But it was what she needed. Time, rather than dulling the grief, worsened it. In the months after Sean's disappearance, when the condolence letters stopped coming and people at the office stopped treating her like a fragile thing, her pain grew deeper, sharper, more focused. What had started as a vague discomfort, an almost-joking sense that this would remain dreadfully surreal until she flew to Nepal and made it real for herself, had become a prophecy. Whether it had always been true or not, the fact was evident now: before she could deal with the pain, she would have to understand what happened.

Knowing was not the same as understanding. She knew the facts, or at least some of them. Sean had signed on for a summit bid of Everest with a small expedition: himself, two other paying clients, and a local Sherpa guide service. His climb was sponsored primarily by a mountaineering magazine that had hired him to write a feature about the experience. It wasn't his first sponsored climb or high-profile feature, but it was his biggest.

Sean ascended the peak on May 11, the first of his group to do so. A fellow climber, Andres Garcia, briefly spoke with him at the summit, the two posing for a photograph together before Sean began the climb back down the mountain.

And that was the last anyone had seen of him.

He never arrived in camp. No other climbers, going either up or down, had seen him or a body that could have been his. There was no disrupted snow, no broken lines, no abandoned gear. It was as if he had simply vanished.

Senseless. Inexplicable. Impossible.

Sean was fit, in the prime of his life. He suffered no injuries or illness on the climb, according to everyone who'd ascended with him. The weather was clear and calm. There was no reason that a man with his climbing talent and experience should have died under those conditions. There was no explanation for how anyone could be lost on a peak as crowded and well-watched as the summit of the world's tallest mountain. Yet that was seemingly exactly what had happened.

Sean Miller had simply climbed a mountain and disappeared.

No one can survive on Everest for long, especially not in the Death Zone near the peak. That was what Carrie had been told when the news was first delivered to her, when she was too overwhelmed by confusion to feel the knife of grief. He'd likely fallen, and his body was probably deep in a crevasse somewhere, or far down the slope, inaccessible and hidden from view by jagged stone and ice. They had explained it to her over and over, so it would sink in that, body or not, he was gone.

He probably died quickly, if it was any consolation.

Unless he hadn't. If he hadn't, he would have died slowly from exposure. A day or two at most was all anyone had ever managed near the peak. Sean was gone. There was no way he would be coming back.

Probably. Most likely.

The uncertainty of it was maddening. It nagged at her in dark hours. Half-formed nightmares of his final moments haunted her, drove her from sleep. She lay awake at night, a hand stretched out into the cool expanse of empty sheets beside her, fingertips moving over the space her husband should have occupied. She stared into the darkness and wondered. And in the dark, doubts grew and doubled and gained a will of their own. Uncertainty became a living creature that shared her body and drove her, against her better judgment, to fixate.

And so, nearly one year after the memorial, she made Tom make good on his promise.

Even among the tourists milling around Lukla, Carrie Miller stands out.

Tall and slender, she looks more like a model or actress than someone planning a summit bid on Everest. She has fine bone structure, with high cheekbones and a straight, thin nose offset by large, dove-gray eyes. Her hair, ash-blond and wavy, has come undone during the long flight, and she looks sleep-rumpled and travel-worn.

Her gear marks her as an amateur. Her backpack and hooded parka are bright and stiff, obviously brand new. Her boots haven't yet been broken in. She stands nervously to the side as porters open the luggage panel of the plane and start pulling out bags, distributing gear among the travelers.

She looks and feels like a new kid on the first day at school, and hates it.

But she hasn't thrown up, and that's an achievement. Now that she's on the ground, her stomach has settled, and her nerves aren't jangling so badly. As long as she doesn't think too far ahead.

Carrie fiddles with the straps on her pack and shifts her attention away from the plane. The airport is just a small building crouched beside the short patch of runway. Beyond, the town unfolds in a surprising burst of color. Buildings with jewel-toned roofs stand in stark contrast to the mountain slope. Prayer flags in red, green, yellow, white, blue flutter on clotheslines strung between buildings.

She's surprised by all the color. In her mind, the Himalayas are nothing but a white-gray expanse of stone and snow. She had almost forgotten that there would be whole towns carved into the mountain slopes. It had not fully occurred to her until now, standing in the middle of it, that Lukla was anything more than a name on a map—that it's a place where people live and work and raise their children, going on with their lives and business just like anywhere else.

This realization should not surprise her, but it does, and that surprise begins to edge out a little of the fear that's taken up residence in her gut.

Looming over everything, though, a sharp contrast to the color and life of the town, are the jagged peaks cutting into the sky. From where she stands, Carrie has to crane her neck to get a glimpse of Everest's peak. Even then, it's mostly hidden from view by cloud cover, a dense fog that tumbles down the mountains. It's like the peak is challenging her, taunting her.

You came all this way to see me, it seems to say. *But I won't make it easy on you.*

Carrie turns away from the mountain, tries to bring her focus back to the moment. She doesn't need to think about the peak right now. She only needs to think one step ahead of her, and that's how she'll get through every part of this journey—one step and one challenge at a time.

Right now, what she needs to do is leave the airport and find Tom.

She heads up the slope toward a cluster of buildings and cobbled path heading into the heart of town. Her pack is only partly filled, and its contents shift awkwardly with each step. It will be better when she's fully geared. Tom will, inevitably, re-pack everything for her anyway, and fuss over every last detail.

That was the agreement when she'd arranged this trip: she would cover the expenses, plus a cash fee to compensate him for his lost wages as a guide this climbing season, and he would handle all of the logistics. They'd negotiated the terms over countless phone calls and emails over the past year, plans slowly morphing from hypothetical scenarios to solid realities. Tom had at first rejected her proposal to pay him for his time. She sent the money anyway. By the time it arrived in his bank account, he at last had to admit she was deadly serious about this plan, and they spent multiple calls back-and-forth hammering out the details in the weeks leading up to her flight out of the country.

"I'm giving you half of this when we get back," he told her.

"If we get back, you deserve twice what I'm paying you," she replied, and smiled like she was joking.

She had offered to meet him in Base Camp, but he resisted.

"I'll see you in Lukla," he told her, and his voice was firm. "It's a two week hike from there to camp. I'm not leaving you to do it on your own."

"Two weeks?" Carrie balked at the suggestion. "It's only like twenty miles."

"Twenty-three miles at an altitude you've never lived in. You can't rush acclimatization. You can't rush any part of this, or it will bite you in the ass." His voice rose with sudden passion. "You're paying me to get up that mountain to look for Sean, but I'm not letting you die up there, too. I won't."

"Maybe if you'd gone with him," she snapped back, and instantly regretted it. Cold silence settled between them, filled only with the vague static of the active phone line.

When Tom spoke again, his voice had been low and even. "I'm guiding you, and you'll listen to me. Think what you will at home. But in Nepal, on that mountain, you'll listen. That's how I'm getting you back in one piece."

She was relieved that the gentleness had evaporated from his demeanor now that he had shifted his role from friend to guide. She didn't need hand-holding on the mountain; she needed someone who could get her up and down the thing in one piece. Tom Fisher the long-time friend might not be the guy for the job, but Tom Fisher the professional mountain guide could be.

CHAPTER TWO

Travel Diary of Sean Miller, dated April 17

Mount Everest is bullshit.

That's what Tom says, anyway. He's been to the summit twice, though, so I don't know if that means I should believe him more or less. Anything can feel over-hyped once you've done it a few times. Humans are nothing if not masters of adaptation, and the bitter downside to that is you can get used to even the most amazing things.

Every day we wake up in a world full of magic. We've sent astronauts into space. We've photographed the depths of the seas and far-distant galaxies. We've mapped out the secrets of the human genome. We've learned to eradicate diseases and grow so much food that governments have to pay farmers to let it rot in the field so world economies don't collapse. The whole of human history is a triumph of exploration and discovery and overcoming adversity, and every day we all pretty much wake up and groan about being tired and shuffle through petty interpersonal melodramas because all the magic of life gets relegated to background noise.

So, yeah, I'm a little bit skeptical when someone who's climbed the world's most famous mountain—twice!—says it's no big deal.

And let's be fair, Tom doesn't mean the mountain itself is bullshit. It really can't be. A mountain is a mountain. It exists, or it doesn't. It's just the things that people attribute to it that may or may not be bullshit, and in this case there is something of a climbing-industrial complex built up around it that, okay, I'll admit, really kind of is some bullshit.

(Note to self: when you write the article, stop saying "bullshit.")

But let the record show: I've heard Tom's criticisms. I have listened. I will even grant that there's some merit to them.

Yes: Everest attracts more commercial attention and inexperienced climbers than any other big mountain in the world. A few dozen people bag the other major peaks every year, a few hundred bag Everest. Many more try.

Yes: Everest isn't a technical challenge the same way as K2 or Annapurna. It doesn't require many feats of mountaineering to navigate its slope.

Yes: Everest has brand recognition. A lot of the clout of climbing it comes purely from people knowing what the hell you're talking about when you say you did it.

It's overrated! It's commercialized! It's crowded and not worth the trouble!

Easy things to say when you've already been to the top of the world.

Look: The mountain may be overrated, but popular things stay that way for a reason. I'm no bearded hipster, ready to walk away from the world's tallest peak just because it's been done before. Which is what I told Tom the last time we discussed making a summit bid together. I knew all the numbers, I'd heard all the complaints, but I wanted to experience it for myself all the same. We'd already climbed Denali and Aconcagua together. I'd made the trek up Kilimanjaro with a different team because Tom was getting paid obscene amounts of money to be a guide that season. That trip went fine. I wished he was there with me— Tom's good, well worth the money he makes at this even if I do give him shit for being a sell-out, and I'd have liked knowing he'd be there to have my back—but the Kilimanjaro team was competent and the climb was good. So with or without Tom Fisher, I can bag a peak. And I will.

(And I'll write all about it in this journal, and then come home and sell my memoir for unfathomable quantities of money, and my future kids will read it some day and say "Wow, Dad, you're a badass!" Hah hah.)

Once I summit Everest, I'll be halfway to completing the Seven Summits—the tallest mountain on each continent. A lifetime's achievement. For all the climbers in the world, all throughout history, less than five hundred people have bagged all seven. And maybe I won't be one of them. Maybe I'll burn out before I get there. But I'm sure as hell going to try. And hey, even if I don't hit all seven before Carrie convinces me to retire, four out of seven isn't half bad—as long as one of the four is Everest.

There was no way around it. I told Tom: I'm going up to Everest, and you can come with me or I'll find a group of my own.

Well. You can guess how that worked out. I'm sitting in Base Camp right now, starting a fresh page in this travel diary. I'm writing too much in it because I'm excited, so don't hold your breath for future entries to be this long. But I do think somebody—those hypothetical kids, future me, even Carrie—is going to appreciate this moment in the future. So I'm savoring it while I've got the energy to write.

Anyway, here I am at Base Camp, and Tom is wasting his God-given talents playing mountain guide for a bunch of tourists hiking through Darjeeling. Sucks to be him.

This mountain has been summited thousands of times since Edmund Hillary and Tenzing Norgay first reached the peak in 1953, but it has never been conquered. That's the thing about big mountains. Other parts of nature can be tamed and bent to human will. Forests can be cut down and rivers dammed up, but you'll never fully domesticate a peak. No matter how many trails are worn into the stone, how many ladders and fixed ropes you install, how much oxygen and food you carry and what high-tech fluorocarbon jacket you wear, the mountain never stops being dangerous. It never stops threatening your life. And that's the beauty of it, the beauty and the danger. That's what makes the mountain call to you, what makes your blood rise with the ache to climb and get a real taste of that pure, sublime power all for yourself.

(Note: That's pretty good. Save that bit for the article intro.)

I wasn't sure how it would feel, for certain, until I got here. I was a little bit afraid even as I trained and packed and bought permits and flew across the world that I'd get here and feel … underwhelmed. Nothing could have been worse than arriving in the shadow of Everest and being disappointed.

But camping here now among the boulders in Base Camp, the peak rising impossibly high overhead, I feel every bit as much awe as I could have hoped. More, if possible. You couldn't understand it without being here. But I have climbed plenty of tall mountains in my life, three of the world's biggest, and none of them have felt quite like this. There is something special about this mountain. I believe that would be true even if it weren't the tallest or most famous; whatever it is, the energy or spirit or whatever you want to call it, that specialness is intrinsic to the ice and stone. That magic was there long before anyone climbed these windswept slopes, long before anyone made a home at its feet. I really believe that to be true.

The mountain goes by many other names given to it by the people who live in its shadow: Chomolungma, "goddess, mother of the world." Deva-dhunga, "Seat of God." Sagarmatha, "goddess of the sky." Everest, by comparison, is an almost embarrassingly banal moniker, named for some Englishman surveyor whose feet never even touched its path. I like to imagine that it was named this way in part from fear, some reflexive attempt to categorize, enforce order, box it in, tame it. And maybe, in some respects, it worked. Mount Everest is certainly not uncharted wilderness anymore. Base Camp is like a party. From my tent right now, I can hear the sounds of music and laughter from one of the big mess tents where beer flows freely and the blue smoke of marijuana builds in a low cloud from illicit joints passed between newly made friends.

There's wi-fi signal at the peak. You could livestream your whole ascent, if you really wanted to, probably.

We've imposed our modern order onto the mountain, the way a surveyor's office once imposed an English name.

But have we tamed it, truly?

I don't believe that for a second.

CHAPTER THREE

Lukla is a riot of sensation, a dizzying blur that threatens to overwhelm the senses.

The relative quiet of the airport has not prepared her for the chaos of the town proper. The streets and buildings seem to fit together poorly, as if the whole thing has been cobbled together at the last minute. It is, anyway, missing the gridlines and angles of Chicago's streets, and the explosion of color is nothing like Chicago's metropolitan gray palette of concrete and steel. It's nothing like Mendoza, either, that Argentinian city in the shadow of its own formidable mountain range. Mendoza had been laid out in a way that, to Carrie, made sense: tall buildings, muted colors, city sprawl giving way to farmland and wilderness in the foothills beneath mountains.

Lukla feels like something different.

To Carrie, still reeling from the long flight and jet-lag and the impending reality of what she's decided to do, the village feels almost hostile. From its frenetic energy and unusual layout to its death-trap airport and the ominously looming mountain peaks, it feels engineered to leave her unsettled.

The buildings here seem to favor simple shapes, all squares and rectangles stacked atop one another, colorful pitched roofs clashing in angle and shade. Painted brick and peeling wood stand side-by-side, buildings smashed together with their awnings leaning over the narrow road like leering mouths. The road itself is more of a path, large flat paving stones heaving upward in an undulating and dusty footpath between shops and hotels and cafes.

Colorful clothing hangs in the front of shops, enticing visitors. A neon-lit pub sign flickers a beckoning light. An internet cafe sits beside a pile of broken stone and rubble. Everywhere she looks is the jarring mismatch of old and new, like she's stumbled into a place caught in time and belonging nowhere.

Or maybe she's the one who's slipped out of time.

There are people everywhere. They crowd into the narrow street, making the open air seem somehow claustrophobic. The smells of pungent spices and dirt and sweat hang in the thin air, a choking combination. Hikers push hurriedly past, packs pulled high on their shoulders, heads held low against their heavy loads. Tourists linger in the street, gawking open-mouthed at the sights as shopkeepers linger beneath their awnings or venture out, calling to passers-by to stop and take a look at their wares.

A cacophony of noise as languages mix and mingle and talk over one another, forming a meaningless wave of sound. Travelers from all over the world, some of them still wobbly in the leg from long flights, stagger around looking for their accommodations. Locals chat among themselves, hurry from place to place, run their shops and their errands or sit and observe the new crop of hopeful outsiders.

Animals, too. That's the most unusual thing. Shaggy yaks, collared in jingling bells, lumber across the path, led by men with weather-worn faces and long, knobby walking sticks. Mongrel dogs, long-legged and scruffy, lie in patches of sunlight or nose through trash piled in the spaces between buildings. Carrie barely manages to jump out of the way of a man on horseback, not hearing the clip-clop of the shaggy mountain pony's hooves until the creature is practically bearing down on her.

Everywhere: Life. Color. Sound.

Under other circumstances, exhilarating. She might have loved it, this vibrant town with its diversity and curious texture. It might have made for a grand adventure in some other time.

But now it is only dizzying, and Carrie presses herself against a rough stone wall and tries to catch her breath. The air is thin, thinner than she's ever experienced, and she pants just with the effort of this short walk from the airport. She has no idea how she will make it to Base Camp like this. How she will climb far enough up the mountain to have a chance of spotting Sean's body.

Her chest is tight, lungs working hard against the elevation, ears ringing in surrender to the noise. It occurs to her, but only dimly, that these sensations might be linked to the bottomed-out feeling in her gut, the tingling in her fingertips, the way her body feels ever-so-slightly alien.

Carrie Miller is not, as a rule, a person who has anxiety attacks.

But then, she is not, as a rule, a person who flies to the other side of the world alone to climb the world's tallest mountain in search of a corpse, either.

Inhale. Two, three, four. Exhale. Two, three, four.

Box breathing, forcing her heart rate to slow, forcing her lungs to expand. Trying to convince her body that she's not drowning. It works, a little.

"Carrie?"

At first she doesn't recognize the voice. Her ears, already working hard at tuning out the din of noise from the bustling street, don't differentiate the words from the collection of unrelated sounds.

But then there's a touch, a hand on her shoulder, and she jerks away from the wall and wheels around, fight-or-flight response activated to 'flight' mode. Her hand drops to her side, where she'd normally carry a purse, where the front pocket would normally cradle a travel-sized can of bear mace.

But there's nothing at her hip.

Her handful of belongings—passport and wallet and street clothes—are tucked in a pocket of the backpack.

This temporary confusion forces her back to the moment, makes her look again at the person who touched her. Recognition settles in place, then relief.

Familiar brown eyes, a feathery shock of mouse-brown hair. A hint of a smile on thin lips, a fine spread of wrinkles at the corner of his mouth and eyes. There's a criss-cross web of fine pale scars on his lips from repeated chapping and peeling. The pinkie and ring fingers on his left hand are missing at the knuckle, lost to frostbite. Tom's in his thirties, the same as her, the same as Sean, but she'd always thought he seemed to have a decade on them. He looks weathered, is why; weathered and used up, prematurely aged.

Sean, by comparison, had always been so full of life. Energetic almost like a little kid.

Ironic, in the end.

"You should have waited at the airport," Tom chides. "I would have met you there."

"I wanted to walk for a while. Alone." It sounds petulant even to her ears, and she grimaces. Averts her gray eyes to study the paving stones underfoot. "It's not what I expected. This place."

A wry smile. "You've only just arrived."

Her head jerks, a partial shrug. She cannot explain what she means. She's traveled before, certainly, spent time in developing nations and small towns hidden at the cusp of wild places. She is no sheltered American, never stepping foot outside her childhood home. She's been to Argentina, where she met Sean for the first time. Japan, where they'd honeymooned. Alaska, when he had summited Denali—she'd flown up to surprise him when he came back down, and they spent a long weekend in Healy recovering before he made the return trip with her to Chicago—and hidden Appalachian villages when he'd taken her on a hiking tour of his childhood, the mountains he'd fallen in in love with, the wild places that had woken something in him. They'd

32

traveled plenty, especially in the beginning when she had been enamored with adventure and he had been eager to show her the world.

So she should not be surprised by unpaved roads and the smell of bodies and animals and foreign spices. She should not be shocked by the mixture of cultures and time periods, this anachronistic melting pot of ancient and new. She should not feel this erratic thumping in her chest, the light-headedness stealing over her with its blanket of dread. She has seen the world. Nepal should not have been a surprise.

All the same, in the brief time since her arrival—hardly more than an hour, surely—she's found it a shock to her senses. Almost offensive.

What had she expected?

She should know better than to think the world would lose its color because Sean was dead, yet some part of her had expected it. She had given Kathmandu a pass when the international flight landed there. She'd been tired and jet-lagged, barely catching a glimpse of the capital city before boarding the plane to Lukla. And then that half-hour flight had stolen all of her courage.

Now here she is, in this town at the seat of the mountain that killed her husband, and she expects … something. Something she cannot name.

"Carrie? You okay?" Tom's hand finds her shoulder again, and this time she lets it stay there.

"I'm fine. Just tired."

"Come get a cup of coffee with me," he offers, stepping away and swinging an arm wide in invitation. "I'll fill you in on everything."

He side-steps, and Carrie realizes he'd come from the building she'd been leaning against. Overhead, a familiar round sign, white letters on a green field: STARBUCKS. Instead of the twin-tailed mermaid, though, there's a mountain at the heart of the circle.

Tom pulls open the door, gesturing for her to come inside, and she swallows back a laugh.

"It's not a real Starbucks," Tom says, sheepishly, almost apologetic. "But the coffee's decent, and the wi-fi is free."

The smell of fresh-roasted coffee hangs in the air, which is otherwise warmed by the proximity of bodies. It's not exactly crowded inside, but it's not as empty as Carrie would have preferred. She slides her bag from her shoulder and hangs it by the door, where it joins many other similar bags on a peg board nailed to one unfinished pine wall.

The cafe is furnished in tightly woven wicker, deep chairs and broad loveseats clustered around low tables. Scattered among the tables and the bar pressed against one wall, travelers sip from paper cups and ceramic mugs and tall, thin cans of beer emblazoned with the shape of the mountain and bearing brands like 'Sherpa Brew.' Mostly, the travelers cluster into small groups. Some read newspapers or leaf through magazines left out on the counter. All of them have glossy photographs of mountains on the cover. Many are printed in languages and scripts that Carrie doesn't recognize.

"I'll go make an order. You want a latte or something?" Tom touches her elbow, leaning in so she can hear him over the general din of the room without raising his voice. His breath is warm against her ear. "Maybe a tallboy?"

"It's a little early for beer," Carrie says. It doesn't sound bad, though. Right now she's desperate for sleep, and a beer would knock her right out.

"On the way home, then," he teases. "We'll stop for a beer before we fly out of here, to celebrate. How's that for a promise?"

His confidence should be charming, but she finds she cannot meet his eyes.

Would Sean have stopped here, she wonders? Would he have stumbled back down the mountain, exhausted but triumphant, to stop for a beer and reminisce? Would he have celebrated with his expedition?

Had the others stopped here? The other clients, the guide, the Sherpas who made it down safe and whole. Did they stop to sleep in a warm bed and sip a latte? Did they gather around these low wicker tables to recount their adventure, sharing stories and celebrating their success even as their team member lay lost and forgotten, dead or dying in the snow?

That line of thinking is torture. She forces herself to shift her attention, casts her gaze around the room for a distraction.

But there's no escaping Everest. It leers at her from every direction. Emblazoned on coffee mugs and beer cans, winking at her from behind the glass of framed photographs adorning every wall. And outside, of course, lurking huge and inescapable, the god she cannot see but knows to be presiding over this town. A crouching and monstrous deity.

Tom returns with two plain coffees and nods toward some chairs in the corner. He hands her a paper cup and she sniffs it experimentally, inhaling the rich scent of dark roast. It smells sweet and milky. She realizes that she has not eaten in hours. Not since the bit of rubbery egg and container of yogurt served up as 'breakfast' on the flight from New York. She should be ravenous, but thinking about food makes her stomach turn.

"How are you, really?" Tom asks, after they've both had a chance to sit and sip their coffees a moment, once it's clear she's not going to say anything of her own volition.

She studies the laminated menu on the table so she can avoid his gaze and his question just a little longer. It lists available drink orders and food on one side. On the other, a few useful phrases in English and Nepali. At the bottom, a note adding that you can ask your server about hiring a guide, porter, or yak for the trek to Base Camp.

"I'm all right," Carrie says, sliding the menu away and at last meeting Tom's weary gaze. "A little jet-lagged. But I'm ready."

"No you're not," he says, the words gentle but cutting in their accuracy. "Not yet you're not. Maybe by the time we get there … " he trails off, then seems to switch gears as if changing what he had planned to say. "It's a long hike. You should be acclimatized a little better by the time we reach Base Camp. And a good night's sleep and some food should help you, too. But I meant what I said before. On the mountain, I'm the boss. You have to listen to me for your safety. You have to trust me completely. You get that, right?"

"I'm paying you for this," she replies, exasperated. "I wouldn't pay for a guide if I wasn't going to listen."

He gives her a skeptical look but doesn't argue. Instead, he takes a long drink from his coffee cup and stares at a patch of wall above her shoulder. There's a faraway look in his eye, like he's gone somewhere else. She turns to look, following his gaze to a photograph of the peak. She doesn't need to ask what's on his mind; it's written all over his face, the tiredness and guilt.

But she doesn't want to talk about Tom's feelings, no more than she wants to talk about her own. Not here, not now, not when she's running on the tail-end of a twenty-hour flight with little sleep and little food. Not when she's already reeling with the enormity of everything. There might be time later for that conversation, to rehash their feelings for the hundredth time, but if he started she wouldn't be able to bear it. She changes the topic.

"So. You've got us a hotel room?"

"Yeah." His attention snaps back to her. "I've got accommodations arranged for the hike up to Base Camp. We spend the night here in Lukla. Tomorrow, Phakding. That'll take about half the day. After that, Namche. We're meeting the rest of the group there."

"The rest ... ?"

"Sherpas. Two porters and a guide."

"You're my guide."

He shakes his head. "I've made it up the mountain a couple of times, but I'm no pro. I'd just ... I feel better having someone with a local agency with us. Besides. We're not here to summit, right? We're here to ... explore, I guess. Search. We need somebody who's comfortable going off the trail and getting back to it in one piece."

"All right. So we meet the team in Namche."

"Right. Two days in Namche Bazaar to make sure we've got everything. By then, I will have been trekking with you a few days and have a better idea of your … um. Style."

"You don't think I'm fit enough."

His gaze slides away from hers again, resting once more on the photo behind her head. He purses his scarred lips.

"I've climbed mountains, Tom. Just because I'm not in your boys club—"

"It's not that." His voice is quiet now, laced through with pain Carrie does not expect to hear. "Just. It's not too late, all right? That's the thing I want to be sure you understand. It's never too late to turn around. Even once we're on the mountain. Even if we're close to the top. You can't do this anymore, and we're done, no questions. Got it?"

"I'm done when I find Sean," she snaps, sharper and louder than she intends.

Noise around them seems to dim. One of those spontaneous silences that happen sometimes, when every conversation coincidentally lulls. Carrie stares hard at the table surface. She feels curious eyes on her but refuses to look up and see who's staring.

"There are services that do things like this. Body retrieval."

"We looked into that already," she replies. And she had, although her heart had never fully been in it. Body retrieval expeditions are difficult to staff and achingly expensive. And, of course, all of the services she had spoken with— over emails, on scratchy international phone calls with Sherpas—had wanted specific details about the body's location and condition. No one wanted to risk their lives tromping around the mountain peak looking for a stranger when they had no idea where to even start with the search.

And besides, other people finding the body won't give her the closure she needs. She has no interest in mortgaging the house just to bring back a frozen corpse. That isn't the point of this, and it never has been. She's here now because she needs to understand. She needs to know exactly what happened, and why, and it needs to feel real to her or else it will haunt her for the rest of her life.

"Let's just take it a day at a time," Tom suggests. His hand crosses the table to touch hers, fingertips brushing the skin on the back of her hand. It tickles. She pulls her hand away and he averts his gaze, wounded.

"After Namche Bazaar?" she prompts, eager to get him back on track.

"Right. So, after Namche. There's Thami, Khumjung, Tengboche, Pheriche, Lobuje." He ticks them off on his fingers. "Six days, give or take. Depending on our pace, and how we're doing with the elevation. Then, well. Base Camp, and we start planning our way up the mountain."

Mountain climbing is not fast. That's something Sean had impressed upon her the first time he'd taken her out hiking. Nothing big or intimidating that first time, just some gentle slopes—a walking trail up the nearest bump in the topography they could drive to in a day trip. Just enough to get her feet wet; his idea of a date. She'd been so enamored with the adventure then, and the intensity of her desire for him had mingled and entwined inextricably with the intoxicating call of the mountains. At the time, she thought she loved mountain climbing. It took years for her to realize that she'd only loved Sean.

But mountain climbing was a slow business. That had been his first lesson. It was the slowest and most methodical of the adrenaline pursuits, a matter more of control and will-power than of heart-pounding risk. It wasn't skydiving or bull-fighting or base-jumping. There was no immediate pay-off, no build-up and dramatic release and temporary, momentary exhilaration. There was only preparation, and training, and ongoing effort.

"If skydiving is like sex," he told her once, when the two of them were at a local climbing wall so she could practice her footing and technique, "mountain climbing is a relationship. You get up onto a mountain and you're not getting back down in a hurry. You're committed to it, whatever happens, good or bad, beautiful or ugly."

She hadn't really understood then, but she thinks now that she finally gets it. If she's serious about this—and by now, after she's come this far, surely she must be—the climb will become her whole life for the next couple of months.

CHAPTER FOUR

Travel Diary of Sean Miller, dated April 19

I spent my whole childhood dreaming about mountains.

The Appalachians were my playground, growing up. They were a place to run away to when staying at home was unbearable. I sought safety in the wild because home was filled with uncertainty and conflict. In the mountains, though, everything is simple: it's just you and your skills and knowledge tested against nature. You live in the moment because you have no other option. You don't have the time to worry about the past or future or anything outside of what you're doing in that very second.

It's hard to explain this passion sometimes, but fortunately I am not alone in it. Climbing is a madness I share with many others around the world, all through history. From the great explorers of bygone eras to the professional mountain guides, weekend warriors, thrill-seekers, survivalists—all of us are linked together by the mountains in our blood. It's the same kind of thing that I imagine connects great authors, writing in the literary traditions of their heroes. Philosophers and great chefs and, hell, even politicians. There's something about being in a community that extends beyond your place and moment in history. Something that transcends time and lets you belong to something so much older and bigger than yourself. And with mountains, part of that thing is as old as the earth itself.

I remember the first time I read a biography of George Mallory, the first man to come close to reaching the summit of Mount Everest. Like a lot of climbers, I admired Mallory for his role in history, but that wasn't the thing that really gave him a special place in my heart. It was the way he talked about climbing. Every quote I could find from him felt like it came straight from my own heart. There, expressed in words, were things I had always felt but couldn't name, and it made me feel less alone.

And that, more than anything, is what brings me here to the roots of Everest, gazing up at the peak.

I missed my chance to go two years ago when Tom made his second summit bid. Climbing is expensive, and Everest is especially costly. I was holding out for a writing assignment that could help defray the costs. Carrie makes most of our money, if I'm being honest, and I think it's unfair to saddle her with an expense like this when I know she wouldn't come and only barely approves. She's always been supportive and downright patient about my climbing, but asking her to fund an expedition just felt like too much.

People who don't climb are often surprised at just how much it costs to do it. There's the airfare, of course, and all of your gear, bottled oxygen, food, fees for your guides and Sherpas, and a climbing permit to even be allowed on the mountain. Nepal's government depends on the income from these permits, just as the local people depend on the income from serving as guides and porters. A huge chunk of the local economy depends entirely on the climbing-and-tourism trade. If Everest was once the goddess of the sky, the mother of the world, perhaps she's still a goddess somehow, watching out for her people, providing—economically, at least, the green language of the modern era.

Regardless, it's not cheap, and climbing to the highest seat of the world isn't something you want to cut corners on.

So I pitched, and waited, and it was worth the wait for this assignment from *Summit Fever* magazine. I'm supposed to climb, and photograph, and write a nice meaty feature about the rise of local guides instead of foreign-based guiding agencies. They're paying most of my expenses. So here's me, recording everything along the way. I've got this journal, the video camera, the disposable camera, the voice recorder, the laptop, the satellite phone. I'd normally feel pretty ridiculous carrying all that crap to the top of a mountain, but if they're paying my bills it's the least I can do. I should probably be typing this actually, to save time later, but I like the feeling of writing long-hand (until it starts cramping; I may have jinxed myself).

Anyway. The goal is to document as much of this journey as I can, for *Summit Fever* and for the book I'd like to write someday, and for myself. Something to look back on. Something to pass along to the next generation. I hope these notes will be turned into something beautiful one day. I hope someone out there ends up reading them with the same love that I had for Mallory's journals when I first checked his book Climbing Everest out of the Logan public library.

Until then, it's nice to have some company on the journey. Climbing is a slow business, especially at this altitude. The acclimatization trips mean that days are spent at lower camps, just watching and waiting for your body to adjust. I'm glad I have this journal to keep me from getting bored.

I say it's nice to have company, but the truth is that you're rarely alone on the mountain. You'd think climbing would be a solitary pastime, but it's a madness shared by many. My own expedition, if you could call it that, consists only of myself and two other climbers—a man from Texas named Warren, I'm not sure if that's a first name or last, and a woman from Connecticut named Susanne Mason, both paying clients like myself. The difference of course is that they're paying their own way rather than being sponsored. Warren is a retired doctor. Susanne does some kind of PR work, something involving television executives and media events. She tried explaining her job to me one night over a few beers in the mess tent, but it didn't make any sense to me. At this altitude, a couple beers may be a couple too many, but I'm not sure I would've followed too well even without the alcohol's unhelpful assistance.

Our guide, Maya Sherpa, is theoretically who I'm here to study for my assignment. Interviewing her and observing her at work is a big part of what *Summit Fever* wants me to do for this assignment. When they told me what they wanted for their feature, it didn't seem like a very big challenge—write an in-depth profile of one of Everest's up-and-coming climbing talents—but now that I've met her I think I can see why they were willing to shell out the cash. She's proving a tough nut to crack.

By all accounts, she's the best in the business as far as Sherpa guides are concerned. She's young, but she's spent over half of her life on the mountain, starting work as a por-ter at age fourteen and never missing a climbing season since. In over a decade of climbing, she's well on her way to setting a summiting record. Despite these impressive achievements, she's not one to talk about herself openly. What I know about her so far, I have mostly gathered from preliminary research. Getting her alone to talk, or getting her to speak candidly about anything, is proving difficult. Her English is quite good, so that's not the problem—it's just that she's laser-focused on climbing and doesn't seem too eager to make small-talk.

I'm going to try to sit her down for a proper interview before we leave Base Camp. I don't think I'll have time once we get up higher.

CHAPTER FIVE

Carrie had met Tom and Sean together at a bar in Argentina. The boys had come to climb Aconcagua, the tallest peak in South America. Carrie had come to study abroad in an over-indulgent summer program that had devolved quickly into an overgrown Spring Break retreat. For a week, she and her friends had spent every night at local clubs, drinking and dancing and seeking questionable hookups with local boys and tourists alike. On that particular night, Carrie was alone at the club. Her friends had left to attend a party with some boys they'd just met, and after a brief but furious debate over their reckless stupidity, she'd refused to follow them. Instead, she stayed behind at the now-comfortingly-familiar club and nursed a brightly colored cocktail while trying not to feel afraid and hurt about being abandoned.

That's when he caught her eye, this tall red-haired stranger, all stringy muscles and knotted joints, a thick smattering of freckles holding together his sun-worn complexion like mortar. He wasn't her usual type, and maybe that's why she felt so drawn to him, like someone answering a primal call. She could tell just by looking at him that he was different from anyone in her life. He was certainly different from anyone in the club. A head taller than most, he towered over the crowd, his skin flushed pink at the cheeks and flaking and peeling off the tip of his nose. He stood like somebody trying not to take up too much space but failing at the task.

He caught her looking at him and, with the kind of lazy nonchalance of a cat sizing up a stranger, ambled toward her. He said something instantly forgettable, maybe because Carrie wasn't paying much attention to his words. But whatever he'd said, it was enough to get them talking, and once he got warmed up Carrie realized she could listen to him all night. The tangle of his copper beard and the way his hair curled around his collar were wild, unkempt, but he spoke in a soft and careful way, and there was a kind of poetry to his words. He sounded like someone from a movie. Or a professor, but the kind who makes the subject captivating.

He bought her another drink. They moved away from the bar, navigating to a quieter booth. There wasn't a live band that night, just tinny speakers piping in out-of-date pop music for the Americans. Carrie was glad for the relative quiet.

"You know, I wasn't going to come tonight," Sean said, gesturing toward her with the neck of his beer bottle. "I hardly ever come to places like this. I actually just agreed to come tonight so I could play wing-man for my buddy Tom. He's the good-looking one, you know."

"Oh, well! If he's the good-looking one, you'll have to introduce me," she teased. She was feeling quite warm. Two drinks at this altitude made for a cheap, happy drunk. "Where is he?"

"Altitude sick," he said, and grinned like he was about to let her in on a scandal. "We're training to climb Aconcagua."

She had no idea what that meant, but she was suddenly very eager to know, and he was more than happy to explain. She got the impression he'd been waiting a very long time for someone to ask him about it. She listened raptly as he explained all about the seven summits and the concept of 'bagging' peaks, about acclimatizing and building endurance and the limits of the human body at an impossible altitude.

She was dazzled. She had never met anyone this interesting in her life. She'd come to Argentina to party and attend a class once in a while; he'd come to conquer the tallest mountain in the Western Hemisphere.

It was impossible not to fall for him.

They'd been talking for quite some time before his companion found their table. Tom, as he was introduced, was shorter and broader, with well-muscled arms and a handsome face. He was also more than a little disheveled and clearly ill; his complexion was grayish, sweat beaded on his forehead and upper lip. His hair stuck up at odd angles, and he smelled like a club bathroom.

"I'd better get him back to the hostel," Sean said, jerking a thumb in his direction. He looked disappointed to cut the night short.

Carrie fished around in her bag for a scrap of paper and a pen. She scrawled her cell number on it and slid it across the table.

"When you come back down the mountain, you'll have to call me and tell me about it," she said, emboldened by drink and conversation and the way his eyes crinkled at the corners.

"I'll do you one better," he replied, and a sheepishness stole over him, a goofy boy-next-door grin. "If you'll let me, I'll come down off the mountain and then I'll show you the whole world."

A summit bid to Aconcagua takes twenty days, and Carrie was certain the boy from the bar would have forgotten all about her in that time. Her study abroad trip was wrapping up and she was sure she'd head home without another encounter. When nearly a month passed with no contact, she assumed he had ghosted her.

But no. As soon as he came back to the valley, she got a call to ask if she was still in Argentina, if she'd like to celebrate with them. Even though her trip abroad was due to end in a couple of days, she hopped a bus to the Mendoza Province to meet up with Sean and his climbing expedition. He was thinner now than he had been the night they met, his beard more tangled and his skin more chapped, but the glow of triumph made up for it.

Tom was looking better, too, and Carrie could see now why Sean had called him the good-looking one. At the time, he lacked his now-permanent tired circles under his eyes and the wrinkles around his mouth. He was almost baby-faced. Back then, he wasn't missing any fingers or toes either.

Carrie wondered then, and again intermittently in the years that followed, how things might have been different if the roles had been reversed. If she'd met Tom first instead of Sean. If Tom hadn't been sick. Would she have fallen for him instead? Or was her attraction to Sean stronger than that, inevitable even?

She was forced to determine that it didn't matter. The window of opportunity had passed. The deal was sealed for her the moment she saw Sean in his post-summit afterglow, that intoxicating air of invincibility and achievement and passion that hung around him like an aura, despite his obvious exhaustion from the physical trial he had endured. She fell in love with him that night the way people fall in love in the movies—hard and fast, without brakes or course-correction.

They dated for a long while after that. Long-distance at first, before he moved to join her in Chicago. Then he moved in with her, at least for the off-season, and it would be years before they were officially married. But in Carrie's mind, she had belonged to him from that night onward.

He had promised to show her the world, and he'd made good on the promise. Their courtship was a whirlwind of travel and hiking and adventure. And while she'd never had his passion or his skill, she'd done a reasonable job of keeping up with him. Sean admitted as much. And Tom had been there often enough to see first-hand that she could hold her own.

She shouldn't have anything left to prove to him.

But all the same, he's been fussing over her like a mother hen the entire time they've been on the trail from Lukla to Namche Bazaar. He's re-packed her backpack and critiqued the way she ties her shoelaces. He's always sending fleeting looks back from the head of the trail. Repeated insistence that they can stop, take a break, there's no rush. Tom is coddling her, and they haven't even reached the real mountain yet.

"You don't think I'll go through with it," she accuses as they stop to eat halfway between Phakding and Namche. They're in an area of flat stones near a suspension bridge, one of many on the trail that criss-cross over sharp cliffs to form foot-paths up otherwise impossible inclines. Bits of colorful cloth, both fresh and falling apart with age, flutter in the wind where they're tied to the bridge's ropes. For luck, Tom tells her the first time she points one out.

"We're taking it one day at a time," he tells her. "I told you—"

"You're the boss on the mountain. I know." She peels the wrapper from an energy bar she's fished from her pack, breaking off a piece with her fingers. She meets his gaze, holds it while she pops the nougat-and-whey-protein amalgamation in her mouth. Chews. Swallows. Runs her tongue over her teeth. It tastes like chocolate sawdust, but it's fuel. "If you think we can spend enough time dicking around in the foothills that I'll get tired or lose my nerve, you're wasting both of our time."

"I'm not." The deep creases around his eyes and the corners of his mouth seem to deepen, as if he's aging right in front of her. "I just want you to be safe."

"Let's go." Carrie shoves the rest of the energy bar in her mouth and starts for the well-worn path. She doesn't look behind her to see if he's keeping pace.

Namche Bazaar is a tiny village, with fewer than 2,000 full-time residents, but it's bustling with life when Carrie and Tom arrive. Backpackers, merchants and livestock crowd together on the path. There are no car-friendly roads up here, and no cars to use them. From here to Base Camp, the most sophisticated form of transportation is yak-drawn cart, and even that is questionable on the uneven pock-marked roads. The forest has thinned, too. For the last day, they've been hiking through thick trees, but now the plants are sparse and scrubby.

From the road, Carrie can clearly see where the treeline stops just ahead on their path. The treeline—that demarcation between life and stone, the last place where nature intends for anything to survive. It's depressingly close, and that doesn't seem to bode well for the rest of their journey.

Namche's narrow, crowded roads and jewel-bright rooftops resemble Lukla, but the geometry is different. Namche Bazaar is carved right into the slope of a mountain, the whole town terraced in rows. It gives the village a curiously one-sided appearance, every building seeming to face the same direction. Buildings fan out in a half-moon, each row higher and offset. All of them seem geared toward outfitting climbers and tourists. Here are shops selling climbing equipment and supplies. Here are signs advertising porters and guides. Here is your last chance, the shops seem to say, to get what you need before you sign your life over to the mountain.

Behind the jagged terrace of Namche Bazaar, a row of mountains rise like ominous bookends. There are many peaks Carrie only vaguely knows the name of: Taboche, Thamserku, Nuptse, Ama Dablam. She could not have pointed out which was which. The only one she's sure of is Everest itself—in part due to the height of its peak, the subtle dominance it holds over the slightly smaller mountains. In larger part because of the feeling of cold dread that settles in her stomach when she looks toward it.

The sun is setting when they arrive, and the orange-gold light reflects off the icy stone wall of Everest's peak, turning it a golden orange. The whole mountain seems to burn.

Tom has arranged a hotel in advance, and he leaves Carrie to get checked in and settled while he attends to some final purchases. He gives an explanation of what he needs, where he's going, but none of it sticks in Carrie's head.

She's too distracted by that looming golden peak, and by the throbbing in her feet, the screaming ache of her calf muscles. She's kept pace well enough all day, but now that she's stopped, a bone-weary exhaustion has crept over her. Their journey has really only just started, but she already feels like she could sleep for a week.

"Take a hot shower," Tom advises, on his way out into the village. "It's the last chance you'll get for a while."

Carrie's hair is still damp when she exits the small upper-story hotel room and heads down to the restaurant in the lobby. She's glad she took Tom's suggestion. The shower was hot indeed, warm enough to spread through her aching joints, and the tiredness of the day-long hike to get here has receded almost completely by the time dinner rolls around.

The hotel has laid out a buffet, warming plates of lentils and curry and rice waiting to be picked over by the hungry climbers and tourists who now fill the lobby. The scent of spices hangs heavy on the air. Carrie's stomach turns at the smell. She's never been a big fan of Indian food, never had the stomach for the strong flavors, but she knows it's best to eat as much as she can tonight. This is the most lavish meal she'll be eating for weeks, and maybe her last chance at a proper hot meal at all. She's not sure what she'll be eating on the mountain, but she imagines it will not be a buffet. More than likely, rations for the foreseeable future will be all grainy protein bars and freeze-dried meals eaten out of foil packets.

It's best to enjoy this while it lasts, even if it's not her first choice.

"Carrie. Hey."

Tom's voice. She turns to see him at a table, waving her over. Seated next to him is a dark-haired woman, obviously a local.

Seeing her, something rises in Carrie's chest, some tense dragon-like specter of doubt and unease. She shifts her course to approach. Tom had made it clear he would be hiring a local guide and Sherpas, but Carrie did not expect any of them to be women.

The Sherpa woman looks older than she probably is, Carrie thinks, examining her well-worn features. She has expressive dark eyes and a prominent bone structure, but her natural beauty is cut through with chafed, leathery skin and deep weariness settled into the wrinkles around her eyes and mouth. Like Tom, she looks used up, prematurely worn out from years of exposure and squinting against the glare of the sun.

She is Carrie's opposite, dark where she is pale, broad and muscular where she is slender, experienced where she is green.

The woman tilts her chin, inclining her head to look at Carrie critically with one nearly-black eye. The restaurant, heavy with the scent of toasted spices and slow-simmered meats, seems to drop in temperature.

Or maybe it's just the blood rushing in Carrie's ears that makes her feel that way. The sudden tingling in her fingers and the prickle of bumps along her forearms.

She feels a smile freeze and turn cold on her face. Her teeth are still bared, like an animal.

The Sherpa woman's eyes are hard and cold.

Tom, caught between them, doesn't seem to understand what's happening or why the air has turned so suddenly hostile. But there's no way he can't know.

When he speaks, it's with the bluster of false cheer, the way somebody speaks when they're eager to change a subject or stop a fight from breaking out. The way someone acts at a holiday dinner when a troublesome uncle has had too many drinks and turned the topic toward politics. "Carrie. This is Maya Sherpa, with the guiding agency I told you about."

His words confirm what Carrie already knows, what she's known in her guts since she caught a first glimpse of her.

Maya Sherpa rises from her seat, reaches out a hand for Carrie to shake.

"Don't you know who this is?" Carrie spits out, ignoring the Sherpa and focusing on Tom. There's no way he doesn't know exactly what he's doing. No way he's not doing this on purpose for some reason. "Of all the fucking guides you could pick—!"

"Look," Tom begins. He licks his lips, gaze darting back and forth. Several people in the hotel are staring at them now. Carrie has not been shy about raising her voice. "Nobody knows the mountain better. She's the best chance you've got at figuring out what happened."

"Because it's her fucking fault," Carrie spits out. The Sherpa woman's hand is thrust in front of her now, and she slaps it away, backpedaling swiftly before she has the opportunity to take a swing at her. "You want me to put my life in the hands of the woman who killed my husband?"

Maya Sherpa says nothing, merely stands there, expression inscrutable, posture frozen.

Tom, too, seems frozen, and Carrie is only peripherally aware of how loud she's being, how many strangers' eyes are upon her. Waitstaff and guests alike are gawking, their curious stares burning into her, but what does she care? Let them rubberneck. She can make a scene if she wants. What difference does it make, at this point? What does she care if a bunch of strangers in the middle of nowhere think she's being rude?

All the same, a part of her—well-buried but well-bred—balks at this flaunting of decorum. Propriety means nothing here in this bizarre funhouse world of color and cold and death, and she's reached her limit. But her upbringing struggles against her emotions, and in the end, the shame wins out.

She turns and stumbles away from them, turning for the door that opens out into the hallway to the lobby. She doesn't know where she plans to go next. There's no escaping this, not really. She's stuck in a strange town in a foreign country. The only way out of this damned town is on foot or by yak, and she's not even certain she could make it back down to Lukla on her own without getting lost.

And besides—if she turns back now, that's it. It's over. She's never getting the answers she seeks, and Sean is staying gone and forgotten forever.

Tom is on her heels. Catches her elbow and spins her around in the hall. "Carrie, stop."

She pulls against his grip, heart thudding, feeling suddenly like a bird with a string tied around its leg. Trapped. Wings beating senselessly, injuring itself in its futility.

Tom's grip tightens. She can imagine her skin bruising under his touch, crushed blood vessels blossoming under her milky white skin.

She stops pulling, but only just.

"I'm sorry I didn't tell you sooner. This wasn't the right way to find out, and that's on me."

Carrie wants very badly to run. She wants, also, to go back into that dining room and lay Maya Sherpa out flat. Knock a few teeth out of her beautiful, weathered face. But she can't do either, not really.

"I think you need some rest," Tom suggests, filling the silence. "Go back up to the room. I'll send some food up for you."

He's not wrong, and she's relieved at the excuse to escape, even if she does feel like a misbehaving child sent to bed without dinner. The solitude of the room is nice, though. She draws the curtains closed, not wanting to see the picturesque view of the looming mountain peak or the sprawling rooftops of the surrounding village. She collapses onto the bed and buries her face into a pillow and lets the tears come.

CHAPTER SIX

Video footage dated April 23

A red-headed figure with freckles and sunburnt skin smiles down into an upturned camera. The angle adjusts as he places it on a tripod. Behind him, a massive boulder painted with the words EVEREST BASE CAMP 5364 M. stands atop a pile of broken stone and white-gray dirt. Beyond, the peak rises in a jagged white slope.

SEAN: Hey guys! Finally got this camera working and to be honest I think I'm leaving it here. It's such a pain to work with! Or maybe I'm just a Luddite. Probably that one! Anyway, though, before I pack it up and leave it for the return trip, I wanted to record a little bit of the journey so far. Mad respect to those documentary crews out there hauling video and sound equipment to the peak!

His grin widens. He thumps his chest twice, then throws a peace sign. He reaches for the camera and the screen is momentarily obscured by his gloved hand. When the hand comes away, the angle has been opened wider.

Standing beside him is a Sherpa woman. Her attention is divided between the camera and Sean, eyes darting back and forth as if nervous or uncertain which to address.

SEAN: This is Maya Sherpa, our Sirdar—that's the senior guide, for you laypeople out there—

MAYA: Who are you talking to?

SEAN: The camera.

MAYA: No, I understand. But who are you making video for? Are you posting to online, or … ?

SEAN: Oh. No. I'm just going to record us talking, to help with my article later. Maybe I'll see if *Summit Fever* wants it for their website or something.

MAYA: So then who are these "laypeople?"

SEAN: … You know, I don't know. Would you like to just answer a few questions for me, then, on record?

MAYA: Okay.

SEAN: First off, how long have you been climbing Everest?

MAYA: Twenty years.

SEAN: Twenty! Really! Wow. That's longer than I would have guessed. You look so young. When did you start?

MAYA: When I was fourteen.

SEAN: Fourteen?

MAYA: Yes. As a porter, helping to carry supplies at the lower camps and clean up after a group moves on higher up the peak. Many from my village choose working this way instead of school. Some stay and become guides, like I did.

SEAN: So how many times have you summited Everest, then?

MAYA: Fifteen. First time, when I was nineteen years old. Then every year after. Every climbing season, I climb, I reach summit. Not every Sirdar can say that.

SEAN: That's true. It's a very impressive track record. And—forgive my saying this—but mountaineering is still often perceived as a male-dominated sport, right? What's it like being a woman in this sphere?

Maya takes a moment to answer. Her attention drifts from Sean to the camera, then back again. Then she shrugs.

MAYA: I don't think that way. I think only like, this is my job. This is how I make money for my family. There are many who see mountaineering as some path to fame, like they are rock stars or something. For me, it's never like that.

Only a thing I am good at doing, and being good with climbing means my brothers and sisters do not need to climb. They can stay in school and become doctors or work in hotel or in the farm fields, whatever they want to be. That's what it means to me.

SEAN: So you don't consider mountaineering to be a passion, then? It's just a job to you?

She shakes her head again.

MAYA: I did not say that. Mountain is my job, but also my home. My whole life is this climbing.

SEAN: I know exactly what you mean.

A voice from off-camera, unintelligible. Sean looks away, off-frame to the right, and nods. Then reaches for the camera, switching it off. There are no other recordings.

CHAPTER SEVEN

Sean was unable to talk about anything else in the weeks leading up to his trip.

"It's just such a cool opportunity," he'd say, by way of bringing it back up, speaking almost shyly as if he had to earn his enthusiasm. "It's really important work, what *Summit Fever* is having me do. There's this whole angle about female empowerment and the local economy and, honestly, this actually seems like something you'd be into with the law firm and—"

"Sean. Do you actually give a shit about any of this, or are you just excited that someone's paying you to climb the mountain?"

He deflated visibly, seeming to shrink down and withdraw. He settled back into his chair, his leather-bound journal cradled against his chest like some small wounded animal.

"I just mean, I don't think it matters what the assignment is, does it? I think you'd be this excited if they were paying you to go up there and, I don't know, measure yak dung or something."

"If it doesn't matter," he said, voice low, "why are you being such a bitch about it?"

The fight that followed lasted long into the night, dredging up all manner of ugliness from the swamp of their shared history. The words exchanged were nothing new—how unfair she was for trying to control him, how she was just trying to make him be realistic, how he had never stood in the way of her ambition, how her ambitions weren't life-threatening, she was jealous, he was obsessed, why didn't they do anything together anymore, why did he only care about climbing, when had she stopped being fun, when was he going to settle down like he'd promised, her window for a safe first pregnancy was closing, didn't he want a family, hadn't they talked about this, hadn't he promised?

In the end, Carrie got all the last words, but it didn't feel like much of a victory. Sean had dropped out of the argument, falling stonily silent, as unyielding and impassive as the mountains he loved so much. Carrie, eager to get a response out of him, angry at his ability to just shut down his reactions and stare unflinching in the face of so much criticism, had begun to raise her voice. She goaded him. She insulted him. She called him childish and selfish and re-minded him that it was her job at the law firm that was pay-ing the bills. That she was on track to make junior partner and she needed a husband she could count on and be proud of, not one she was ashamed to introduce to her boss be-cause he was a stupid, thrill-seeking man-child with a death wish.

This was not the first time they'd had this argument, but it was the last time they ever would.

In the light of what had happened, every detail of the fight gained a dreadful significance, an unbearable leaden weight that would surprise Carrie in quiet moments, crush her as she struggled to sleep. She could remember every word, and she thought that at the end of her life, every one of those cruel things would be stacked on a scale and she would be forced to reckon with their weight.

That night, he went to bed on the couch, which was the opposite of what she wanted. What she actually wanted—needed, but had no way to ask for—was reassurance. All she wanted was for him to hold her close and tell her that he still loved her, to run those large callused hands over her body or smooth back her hair and whisper some affirmation.

They had thrown a going-away party, a dinner with a few close friends—everyone but Tom, who was on the other side of the world—and gotten drunk on the good champagne. And once everyone left they'd fallen into bed together and had the kind of mind-blowing make-up sex that was electric-charged with tension and passion and anger and love, and he'd been so dead asleep he missed the first alarm and almost been late for his flight out. They kissed at the airport and made jokes, and at the time it had all felt like it would be okay.

Looking back, she'd like to say that some twisting sick dread had filled her as he walked through the gates toward security.

But in truth, she'd felt nothing. If anything, she had felt relief: *The fighting is over now. He'll climb the mountain, cross it off his bucket list, and finally be ready to put it to rest. Finally, we can start building a life together without Everest hanging over our heads.*

And for a little while, it seemed like that would be true. She got emails from him, little travel updates whenever he could snag some wi-fi. He called her once or twice from the satellite phones at camp, just to hear her voice, however far away and time-delayed the conversations were—like talking to someone on the moon, waiting for the signal to transmit, a conversation stretched out away from real time.

But then the contact ended, and there was only silence while he pushed toward his final ascent.

And then the phone call, just as she was sitting down for dinner, leftovers for one and a glass of wine in front of mindless primetime TV. They say bad news always comes in the dead of night, but it had been evening there, and morning on the other side of the world; Nepal's time zone was inverted, a mirror image.

There's been an accident.

She barely heard a word of it the first time. Her head felt like it was full of bees, an insistent buzzing that drowned out the explanation. Afterward, she could not remember who had called her, or what their voice had sounded like, or really what was said.

Had it been Maya Sherpa, the woman who had guided him up the mountain? Had she called that day to take responsibility for her role in his death? Or had it been someone else, someone he'd climbed with, a doctor at Base Camp, some person sitting back in the guide agency who had never even been to the top of the mountain? She didn't know.

She must have talked to other people afterward—someone from the embassy, surely. Somehow she'd made arrangements, gotten some belongings shipped back. But she couldn't really remember any of it. The whole thing was a blur, partly shrouded in grief, partly in a haze of alcohol and sleep. Somewhere along the way, the conversations were taken from her, shuffled off like everything else: paperwork, funeral planning, bills, her caseload at work. For a little while, she had simply ceased to function, and looking back, the memories for those days, weeks, were so much empty space.

But she knew one thing for certain, because it was a part of an argument that had been etched indelibly into her memory, gone over countless times, reinforced by the video she'd found in his belongings that had been recovered and shipped to her.

That last, final glimpse of his face, the last recording of his voice. The final moments of his life that still existed, and all of it was dedicated to that guide—the woman Sean had been paid to profile, the woman who had spent weeks with him on the mountain, who had abandoned him to die—Maya Sherpa.

Carrie has always hated crying. Hates it because it makes her feel weak and gross. In the movies, women can be tragically beautiful when they weep, but in Carrie's experience there is no beautiful sadness. Only snot and puffy eyes and contorted, awkward grimaces. She hates it, too, because she knows how easy it is to weaponize tears. She watched her mother do it all through her childhood, fits of histrionics that always managed to turn the tide in her favor, that ensured the spotlight and special accommodations never wavered. Carrie never wanted the same treatment. If she was going to get something, she wanted to earn it, and feel accomplished for earning it—not feel the hollow victory of manipulation.

All the same, there's no fighting the grief and anger and embarrassment and confusion that have built up and spilled over in salty rivulets, and she gives in to them until she's exhausted.

The memory of Tom's fingers is bruised into her arm.

She looks around the hotel room for a clock, some indication of how much time has passed, but she doesn't see one. She should go back down there, she knows. Talk to Tom. Apologize, probably, to him. To Maya. If she's going to do this thing—if she's really, truly going to do it—then her life is going to be in their hands, and she needs to make peace with that. Needs to be okay with trusting them.

But if she apologizes, she knows it won't be genuine. She's emptied of tears, but the hurt still festers, deep down.

A knock at the door. Carrie frowns, sitting up from the bed.

"One second," she calls, and hurries across the room to the little sink, splashing cold water on her face and scrubbing her cheeks. She pats her face and hands dry and meets her own gaze in the spotted, slightly warped mirror. Takes a deep breath. Tries to compose herself.

Get it together, Carrie Miller.

When she opens the door, she is surprised to see Maya Sherpa standing there, even though she can't really imagine who else it would have been. Maya's dark eyes settle on her, her expression as stony and unreadable as the face of the mountain.

'Calm' has never been one of Carrie's finer qualities.

Even in the courtroom, no one could accuse her of keeping a level head. She could manage decorum, could play by the rules, but at the end of the day, she's carved an identity for herself from bullish tenacity. Unafraid to speak her mind and unwilling to back down—that's her brand. Calm and steadfast? That isn't her. It never has been. She's never wanted it to be.

But now, in this moment, she feels a pull of terrible envy for Maya Sherpa and her impenetrable calm.

"Your husband was a good man," Maya says. Her accent is thick, but her English is clear. "A strong climber, too. But a bad listener."

Carrie's voice comes out more choked and shrill than she'd have liked. "Are you saying what happened was his fault?"

Maya shrugs. "Who can say? No one knows but the mountain, and she does not give up her secrets." She hesitates, then pulls a small, battered leather journal from a pocket of her puffy climbing pants. She holds it out for Carrie. "Maybe you find your answers here."

Carrie takes the journal, frowning. It's weathered, the edges worn down and wrinkled. The whole of it seems to curve slightly, as if molded from a long time carried in a back pocket. But it's immediately distinctive. There are dozens of them at home, the same size, soft leather bindings wrapping up countless field notes and daily scribblings. They fill a box that Carrie keeps tucked away deep in a closet because it hurts too much to look at them.

"That's Sean's," she says, dumbly, and holds it to her chest. Turns a protective shoulder toward Maya, as if worried the Sherpa woman will have seconds thoughts about handing it over. Like she imagines she'll lunge for her and snatch it away. "This is one of Sean's notebooks."

Maya nods.

"Why wasn't it with the rest of his stuff? Why do you have it?"

"Carrie, calm down." Tom, coming down the hall, a take-out box in hand. He comes up behind Maya, who takes a step sideways, allowing him passage into the hotel room. "Not everything got shipped back to you. You know that. There are a lot of supplies on an expedition. Things get jumbled up."

"Did you know about this?" She rounds on him. Takes a step back, retreating further into the room. She's hugging the journal to her chest now with both arms, her pulse quickening.

"Not … not until recently," Tom says, hesitantly. His gaze lands on the floor, either from guilt or just trying to evade Carrie's harsh look. "It didn't come up. Look, Carrie, I didn't … I don't know what's going on in your head sometimes. But I promise you, I'm not trying to do anything to make you angry. I'm gonna need you to get it together."

He looks up. Glances at Maya, who inclines her head, a little half-shrug that seems to communicate, *This is a 'you' problem*. His gaze turns back to Carrie.

"You wanted to do this, so we're doing it. Maya is an expert guide. She was the last person to see Sean alive. If you're serious about wanting to know what happened up there, if you really want to find him, it's got to be this way. If not? If you can't handle this? You need to tell me, and you need to be honest. Because I know you're hurting, but if you pull any bullshit on that mountain, you could get yourself or someone else killed. I need to know you understand that."

Carrie exhales. It's a relief, somehow, hearing him talk like this. It's what she needs from him—not gentleness, not sympathy. Tom the mountain guide. The professional. It steadies her nerves.

"What time do we leave tomorrow?"

"Six." Tom hesitates, like he's not sure whether to push it or accept her question as acknowledgment of what he's said. "It'll take us a week or so to get to Base Camp. We can't speed that part up unless you want to flirt with altitude sickness."

"Okay. Six. I'll be ready." She looks between Tom and Maya. Swallows down her pride. Says out loud what has to be said, as much for her as the two of them. "No bullshit. All business."

Tom holds up the takeout box. "You should eat tonight. You'll be missing hot meals soon enough."

She nods toward the general direction of her bedside table, gesturing for him to set it down. "I will in a minute." Her attention flicks back to Maya. She tries to smile, holding up the journal. "Thank you for giving this to me," she forces herself to say. "Have you read it?"

Maya shakes her head. "Can't read English. Only speak."

Carrie isn't sure whether she believes that, but decides it's best to pretend she does. "Well. Thank you. I'm … going to get ready for tomorrow. Six am."

"Six am," Maya agrees, and steps away from the door, shuffling down the hall.

Carrie wishes Tom would go with her. The journal smells of leather and book glue and Sean. She wants to be alone with it, wants to spend the night poring over it, drinking in every last word he's left behind for her. But she feels Tom's gaze on her, and she retreats to the bed instead, folding herself up onto the twin-size mattress. She sits cross-legged in the center of the bed, the takeout box in her lap, the journal on the bedspread next to her. Runs a finger over the leather, touches the places where it's been worn smooth by friction. Imagines it in Sean's pocket, molding to the curve of his body.

Closes her eyes, tries to remember how it felt to lie in bed with him at her back, his strong arm wrapped around her, a warm hand laid over her breast.

Feels Tom's gaze on her.

Opens her eyes, goes back to eating. Avoids looking up. She shovels spoonfuls of spiced lentils and rice into her mouth and swallows them down, and eventually Tom retreats to the bathroom to take his own advice about showering.

Before he emerges, Carrie deposits the remainder of her food in the trash and climbs down under the covers, bringing the journal with her. She turns her face toward the wall and does not move when Tom emerges.

"Hey," he says, in a low voice, a half-whisper. "Are you up?"

She doesn't reply. Listens. Hears him settle into the bed opposite hers, the creak of bed springs and the rustle of fabric. Hesitant breathing—frequent, sharp inhales, as if preparing to speak, then letting it go, changing his mind.

Only when she hears him snoring does she allow herself to sleep, the travel diary cradled in her arms like a teddy bear.

CHAPTER EIGHT

Sean's travel diary, dated April 28

Well, the camera has already died. I'm leaving it at camp to collect on the way down. I don't know what happened. Something is draining the batteries so quickly. They won't hold a charge at all. All the expedition's electronics are going on the fritz actually. Maybe it's the cold. Bad luck. Ionic wind? Whatever it is, I hope it doesn't start fucking with the oxygen tanks, but those are way lower-tech.

See, this is why pen-and-paper journals are the way to go! (Future generations, take note.)

The Sherpas are preparing for their puja ceremony now. A Buddhist lama has made the trek here from one of the temples to complete it. Everyone, climbers and Sherpa support alike, participates. I'm excited to see what it's like. My understanding is there will be prayer, to ask the goddess of the mountain permission to climb and for safe passage to the summit. The Sherpas won't climb without it, I'm told.

Here's a bit of trivia for the memoir (maybe *Summit Fever* will be interested too):

Before English mountaineers first arrived in Tibet—Nepal was not accessible to outsiders at that time, so the mountain had to be climbed from the North side—no one had thought to climb the peak. I always thought that was funny. For the people of Tibet and Nepal, the people who live in the Himalayas among the towering peaks, there was never any urge to climb and conquer. They told stories about the mountain, built a place for it in religion and superstition, lived in its shadow and valued its role in their weather and lives. But never climbed it.

When asked why he wanted to climb Mt. Everest, George Mallory reportedly replied, "Because it's there."

Two kinds of people.

Mallory's answer seems glib, almost flippant. Moreso if you've never stood in the shadow of a great peak. The mountain calls to you. It gets in your blood and whispers taunts and promises. You climb the peak because to not do so is incomprehensible.

Why do we do anything? Why eat, or fuck, or pull our hand away from a burning flame? These actions are in our nature, written there indelibly. Once Everest gets into your blood, you have no choice but to answer its call.

So Mallory, I can understand. The people who stood in its shadow and ignored that summons for centuries, that's harder for me to imagine. Didn't anyone ever get curious? Didn't they ever feel that same magnetic draw to stand atop the world?

Either way, Mallory never achieved his goal. At least, as far as anyone knows.

He attempted the summit three times in his life. The first two were failures. His third attempt is a mystery. He and his partner, Andrew Irvine, were seen cresting toward the summit, visible within 1,000 feet of the top. Then they disappeared from view, never to be seen again. Seventy years later, climbers found his body—vomited up, perhaps, by a mountain that no longer had need for it. Did they make it, before they died? Did they reach the summit? Or did they fall short, doomed to spend an eternity just out of reach of their goal?

I don't know. No one does. No one's even found Irvine's body, or the camera he was carrying that could have given some proof about what happened in those final hours. It's one of the mountain's greatest mysteries, the kind of ghost story climbers tell one another.

I won't have a chance of finding Irvine's body on this trip. That's a mystery that will have to be left to someone else. I'm taking the Southern route, the one Sir Edmund Hillary climbed in the first documented successful ascent of the mountain—1953, a full thirty years after Mallory's doomed attempts. I didn't really plan it that way. But I guess it feels auspicious, if you're going to make the climb, to follow the footsteps of the man who survived.

I hope some of Hillary's luck is still here on this mountain.

Anyway. The puja is starting. I wish I could get the camera working so I could document it. I hope there's food involved.

We leave Base Camp in the morning!

CHAPTER NINE

In the morning, they meet with two more Sherpas. These two will be acting as porters, Tom explains; they'll help carry supplies and set up and tear down the camps as they progress up the mountain. The two he hires are named Pemba and Lopsang. No last names, like pop idols. Or maybe Pemba and Lopsang are the surnames, like a pair of secret agents. Carrie isn't sure and is too embarrassed to ask. She's already struggling to wrap her head around how 'Sherpa' can be an ethnicity, a job title and a surname all in one.

How is she supposed to act around the porters? She doesn't know how to ask that question, either, without betraying her ignorance. Are they more like coworkers, or serving staff? Is it more polite to ignore them while they go about their work, or is she supposed to show gratitude each time? It's a small, sharp reminder of how much Carrie doesn't know about big-time mountaineering. How painfully obvious it is that her experience has all been child's play.

Not knowing how to treat the porters, she settles instead on observing them.

Pemba is an easy-going man in his early twenties. He's quick to laugh and frequently has a joke ready. Lopsang is taller, probably older, and prefers to hang back at the tail end of the group, watching quietly from the rear.

The five of them begin the trek to Base Camp. For Carrie, it's more of the same: slow, steady hiking over stony inclines, stopping frequently to rest as her lungs struggle to adjust to the atmosphere. The difficulty makes a mockery of the distance. A six-mile journey eats up a day's efforts. Namche Bazaar to Tengboche, with its tea house and Buddhist temple, the light dust of grass growing over its terraced ground. Tengboche to Dingboche, where the grass grows even more sparsely, stones and ancient earth overtaking the landscape. Dingboche to Lobuche, a tiny collection of buildings, nothing that could be called a town. And then onward, over boulders and dusty paths, through Gorak Shep and up to Base Camp itself. Less than twenty miles of hiking, spooled out painstakingly over several slow-moving days.

All the same, Carrie finds that she prefers these wild parts of Nepal, the rocky slopes and forested paths, to the riots of color and jumbles of uneven streets in the towns. It's quieter in these empty stretches. Not so crowded or busy. Though they do occasionally run into other groups making their way up the same trails: climbing expeditions with gear loaded onto the back of yaks, porters bent double against the weight of their loads. Families, too, even children with bright backpacks and scarves, their parents posing them for photos in front of boulders or at shrines along the way.

"They're just trekking to Base Camp," Tom reassures her, catching her expression as her gaze follows a group. They've stopped to break and eat in a sunny patch of trail. Lopsang is making tea—necessary for both hydration and warmth, but lacking in flavor—and Carrie's been watching their fellow hikers the whole time.

But Tom has misunderstood. It's not concern that draws Carrie's eye to these high-altitude vacationers. Rather a deep, physical longing, a wistful ache for what might have been. Looking at the group of them taking selfies in front of a patch of yellow wildflowers peeking out from around a boulder, Carrie tries to imagine being there under those circumstances rather than her own.

Her and Sean and some pale-haired, freckled child between them, traveling the world, conquering mountains.

Sending Christmas cards back home to her family with bold snapshots of the three of them standing on top of the world.

If she hadn't tried to stop Sean from climbing—if she hadn't been so insistent that he retire, settle, think of their future—would he have lived?

Or would they have all three died out here together, a family tragedy at 18,000 feet?

Their arrival at Base Camp catches Carrie almost by surprise. On one level, she knew, of course, that they'd been getting close. Each day's trek, painstakingly slow as they had been, brought them further into the mountain's shadow. They left forests behind them, then grass and wildflowers, until all that was left was dirt and stone, the mountain's ever-snowy peak a constant presence ahead of them. They passed, from time to time, a Buddhist shrine or a stone wall curiously inscribed with letters she could not read. Otherwise, the path felt increasingly lonely as it wound its way up to the mountain. Even when they passed other hikers on the trail, there was a sense of isolation that had not been present closer to the towns—like the whole area was holding its breath in anticipation of something.

Now, the mountain's peak—a constant looming presence at the lower elevation—is especially foreboding. Carrie has to crane her neck to see the top, squinting against the brilliant gleam of its white slopes.

Ahead on the path, a large and battered yellow sign reads quite simply: WAY TO M.T. EVEREST B.C.

She nearly laughs at the sight of it, laughter borne from its incongruous absurdity. It states the obvious with such cheerful frankness . But it drives home, too, a thing that she's almost forgotten over the past several days: she's really doing this. No longer preparing to climb the mountain anymore, but actually doing it. In a few short steps she will be on the mountain itself, will be part of it.

"We're here," she says, staring at the sign and feeling the enormity of the task before them catch up to her all at once. "We're doing this."

She hears the incredulity in her voice. Wishes it isn't there.

"A lot of people only make it this far," Tom says, cautiously. She's sure he thinks he's disguised the optimism in his voice, as if she doesn't know that he's woken up every day of this journey so far hoping she'll decide she's had enough.

"It's better that way," Maya interjects. She's rooting around in one of the packs, looking for something, and doesn't bother to look up at the others when she speaks. "Tourists come, stay in camp. Feel they have seen Everest. Maybe it's enough. Keeps them from trying the summit."

Despite herself, Carrie's curiosity is piqued. She turns away from the sign. "Isn't it better for you if more people want to summit? For your business, I mean."

Maya shrugs. Pulls a candy bar out of the pack and begins unwrapping it. "Only so many can summit each year. Summit window is only good three, four days."

"A lot of people try to climb Everest who have no business doing it," Tom explains, then winces. Present company excluded, he might have added, but doesn't. He pushes past the point hurriedly. "I get what she's saying. You look at a really difficult peak like K2, and there's only been a few hundred people to ever summit it. It might get fifty attempts in a really big year. Everest has easily ten times that, and double or triple as many gawkers milling around Base Camp."

Carrie's brows lift. "Everest isn't difficult?"

"I didn't say that." Tom sighs, exhaling a foggy breath as his gaze rolls upward, straying toward the peak and the too-blue sky surrounding it.

"No one wants to climb K2," Maya says, shrewdly. She breaks the candy bar in half and takes a bite from one side, chewing it indulgently, swallowing, running her tongue over her teeth before she continues. "What is it you say in the West? 'Such and such is my personal Everest?'" The disgust in her voice is palpable. She meets Carrie's gaze, her mouth twisting in a wry smile. "You do not hear 'My personal Ama Dablam' or 'my Makalu.'"

Pemba snickers. Lopsang nudges him, shooting a questioning look, and Pemba quickly translates, repeating the joke in their native language. Lopsang snorts.

Maya rises to her feet, finishing the other half of the candy bar and shaking her head. "You Westerners think that you name a thing, you own it. Why should you not climb? So you do, and each year, some die."

Carrie's cheeks go warm, blood rushing toward them as a coil of anger tightens her gut. She cannot help but think of Sean, imagining the look in his eyes when she kissed him goodbye at the airport, the frozen smile on the photograph sitting on the easel at the memorial service, ringed in flowers. *How dare she?* Carrie sets her jaw against a sudden urge to lash out at the woman. *How dare she talk about him that way?*

But Tom, perhaps sensing the shift in mood, moves hurriedly to stand between them, blocking the path. He lays a hand on Carrie's back, prodding her forward. "We should get going. We have tents to set up and plans to go over. Come on."

She shrugs off his hand but follows his lead, passing the battered orange sign with its helpful arrow. The others fall into step around her, and if Maya has more to say, she doesn't say it aloud.

Base Camp is a mismatch of starkness and warmth, color and bleak gray stone. This far above the treeline, the mountain is as alien and inhospitable as the surface of the moon. There's no sign of natural life here, only white-gray boulders jutting up from frost-hardened blackish-gray earth littered in bits of broken stone. The natural palette is grayscale, like an old-time photograph, with only the blue sky to offer any contrast.

But overlaid onto this monochromatic landscape is an explosion of color. Tents of brilliant gem-toned nylon flutter in the wind. Bodies dressed in bright, puffy jackets mill around in crowds. Animals wander untethered through the camp, incongruous against the harsh landscape.

In the foothills and forests, animals range wild—deer and snow leopards and lion-maned goats called tahr. But nothing lives naturally on the peak; the mountain is incompatible with life.

Yet people insist on bringing life with them wherever they go.

There are probably a dozen domestic yaks milling around camp, nosing hopefully among the stones for something to eat. Pack animals hired at lower altitudes are handed off to those who will tend to them until it is time to send them back to town. There's no use for them at this altitude; the path from here to the summit is too narrow and treacherous even for the mountain beasts.

A skinny mongrel dog skirts around the perimeter of camp, sniffing experimentally at tent stakes and hiking its leg against the side of one bright blue tent. Carrie isn't sure whether anyone owns the dog, if it's been brought here on purpose or if it somehow simply wandered up here in hopes of finding scraps of food among the campers. Surely there are better places to beg, but he seems content enough, scratching at an ear before flopping down in a sunny patch of ground.

The overall atmosphere at Base Camp is less somber than Carrie had expected. When she was a freshman in college, she'd joined with a group of sorority sisters and caravaned to Burning Man; that's the closest thing she has to compare camp to now. Tents are set up haphazardly in the shadow of boulders, built in areas flattened by centuries-old glaciers that have come and gone and left smooth patches in the earth. Most tents are small domes, built to withstand wind and cold, but some are large and house-shaped: mess tents, supply tents, communal spaces for eating and drinking and socializing.

Like Tom had said, many of the people at camp seem to have no interest in going any further up the slope. There's a celebratory air among some of these sightseers; for them, their journey is over, culminating triumphantly at the foot of Everest. The family Carrie had seen on the path—mom and dad and two blonde-haired children whose pink faces barely peek out between knit caps and fuzzy scarves, their bodies obscured by puffy jackets—are eating together in an open-air picnic. They'll stay a night or two, Carrie imagines, then pack it up to descend the mountain again, taking their snapshots and memories and sense of accomplishment home again.

She burns with jealousy, watching them, as she fumbles with the stakes and straps of her tent. How simple it must be, to be them: they came, they saw, they got away.

Why wasn't that enough? Why couldn't that be enough for her?

And why hadn't it been enough for Sean?

"Carrie," Tom's voice, gentle at her back. "We have Sherpas to do that. Come take a break for a while."

She bristles, shrugging away the touch of fingertips at her shoulder. She edges sideways, glancing up and over her shoulder to meet his gaze. "I can set up my own tent."

"I never said you couldn't." He sighs. "Look. The entire reason we pay porters to carry supplies and set up camp is so that you can save your energy. You'll need every ounce of it."

"No one carries things for them."

He chuckles at that. "Christ, you sound just like Sean sometimes." He touches two fingertips to his forehead, a long-suffering and wearied gesture. "Tell you what. We can argue about Sherpa rights all you want once we get off the mountain. I'm sure Maya would have lots of opinions for you as well. But for right now, the point is that they are used to being here, and you're not. Your body's going to be burning every bit of energy it has just trying not to die from the altitude, and it's only going to get worse from here. So don't waste any of that energy on shit you don't need to do, all right?"

She grumbles, but agrees, grudgingly stepping away from the partly-erected tent. She doesn't know how to explain that she needs the distraction. Needs to feel busy, in control of something. That without something to keep her hands and mind busy, she'll be dragged down into an abyss in her thoughts—that focusing on the here and now is the only thing keeping her from falling into the limitless void of 'what ifs' and uncertainty.

She realizes, with a bitter smile, that Sean had explained something similar to her on more than one occasion.

Would he be proud, she wonders?

Would it make him happy to know that, at last, she understood how it feels to run to the mountains instead of confronting her troubles head-on?

The second day Carrie is at Base Camp, the Sherpas and climbing teams assemble outside the mess tent for something called a puja ceremony.

"I don't suppose this is the kind of thing I can sleep through?" she asks Tom, only half-joking. The idea of being around others, of being surrounded by strangers and feeling the buzz of their excitement and ambition, makes her stomach churn.

"It's not," Tom confirms. "There's food, though. Come on."

She casts a longing glance over her shoulder at her tent and sighs, then follows Tom to join the messy circle that's assembled outside. In the center of the grouping is a stack of climbing gear – axes, climbing harnesses and ropes, crampons, even oxygen bottles. Beside that is an altar of piled stones, draped in brightly colored prayer flags. There are pictures and bowls of fruit and snacks all over it.

"What is all this?" she asks, speaking low so no one will hear her inexperience.

"A Buddhist lama comes and blesses the climbing equipment," Tom explains, gesturing with his chin. "And then prays for safe passage for all of the climbing teams."

"And they do this every year?"

"Every year. The Sherpas won't climb without the blessing."

"It's not exactly fool proof then, is it?"

That is, of course, the moment that Maya appears, burrowing between them carrying an armful of gear. Carrie winces and looks away, trying to evade the Sherpa woman's gaze, but she feels the dark eyes boring into her anyway.

"We ask for blessing and permission," Maya says. "Whether the Goddess grants what we ask, is something different."

Maya hurries past before Carrie can form a fitting response. She is, frankly, relieved. She does not want to discuss the mortal accounting of capricious gods with anyone, much less the Sherpa woman who she will be trapped with for weeks in this frozen purgatory.

"Just follow my lead," Tom instructs, as the ceremony gets underway.

She goes through the motions, bowing her head when it seems appropriate, taking the food and drink that is offered. Even puts up with the flour that's dusted on her cheeks, symbolizing a beard of old age. She doesn't think it looks much like a beard. Looking around the assembled climbers and Sherpas, she sees dozens of faces dusted with flour, their skin now gray and ashen like corpses. The crowd has morphed, grotesquely, into an assembly of ghosts, and no-body else seems to have realized it.

Sherpas form a line and begin a ritual dance. Carrie digs deep in herself, tries to find a glowing ember of hope or excitement or even simple curiosity at the culture on display. But all she can dredge up is cold, knotted dread.

Tom's acclimatization schedule demands that they stay for several days at Base Camp before moving on to the next camp. It will be like that for the rest of their journey: a few hours of active climbing, then a long rest to recuperate and acclimatize before moving on. It's essential, Tom explains, for allowing their lungs and hearts to get used to the stress of the higher elevation. Rushing the acclimatization is a sure recipe for death and disaster.

A part of Carrie wants to get on with it, to hurry toward the peak and reach the elevation where they can begin looking for Sean. But the rest of her is bone-weary and exhausted with the effort of breathing, and she's relieved that this is an expected response, not a sign of impossible-to-overcome weakness.

Despite herself, she gets to know many of the other climbers in camp. It's hard to avoid them, with the tents so squashed together, the shared mess tents, the latrines dug in trenches in the frozen earth. There's an intimacy among strangers on a mountain, even among strangers whose goals differ, whose lives will never intersect again.

There are several disparate groups of sightseers. The family and their scarf-wearing children left soon after arrival, but plenty of other backpackers have stayed to mill around camp for days, seemingly just to soak up the ambiance. One long-haired man in his twenties likes to sit out on a boulder in the afternoon and strum a battered old guitar, crooning lyrics from Bob Dylan or Paul Simon. He's a better guitar player than vocalist, and not particularly good at either, but against the dark and the cold and the bitter silence of the mountain, there's something comforting about his performance all the same. Carrie know she'll miss him when she moves on to the next camp.

There's an expedition from Japan planning a summit bid. They chatter frequently in Japanese, often carrying on conversations excitedly, loudly, back-and-forth discussions that make her dizzy to overhear. Carrie can pick out only the occasional familiar word or phrase, her Japanese woefully inept from the brief studies she'd made before her honeymoon—ages ago, now, knowledge that belonged to a past self, someone who is no longer a part of her. When she does recognize words, they come to her with a surprising jolt, like waking voices cutting through into a dream.

There's a multi-national expedition, too, led by a German guide. Carrie gets the impression he's kind of a big deal in climbing circles, although she's never heard of him. He carries himself like someone important, though, and he's here on some kind of corporate sponsorship, maybe planning to break some kind of record or do something gimmicky for clout. Some of the people attached to his group seem like reporters, sharp-nosed and insistent as rodents. Carrie avoids the whole crowd of them instinctively. The last thing she needs is media attention for what she's doing.

She can all too easily imagine it, the fake curiosity in their voices: *So you're here looking for your dead husband? But you never received confirmation that he had died? A body was never found? Do you believe that he may still be alive? Do you plan to bring the body home with you? Why not pay a team to do it for you? Do you feel like it's worth the risk to make the climb yourself?*

Just imagining it makes anger rise white-hot to the surface, and she finds herself spending more time in her tent, resting or fussing over plans with Tom or, when no one is likely to interrupt her, reading Sean's diary. Anything to avoid conversation with the others.

Sean's travel journal, at least, proves to be a safe refuge. Reading it makes her feel like he's here with her, whispering in her ear when she settles in for sleep. His voice, or what she remembers of his voice, sets up residence in her head. The journal sounds just like him, like he'd written every word as a message for her.

He had always been more expressive on the page than in person. It was part of his charm. In person, he would often stumble through awkward attempts at conversation and sheepish, halting proclamations. But in writing, he was all poetry. When they were first dating, he'd send her long handwritten letters lovingly folded into nice envelopes and mailed to her college dorm room.

"Haven't you heard of email?" she'd teased, but she was secretly pleased. Letters were realer, truer somehow than words on a screen, and receiving them—these things he had touched and labored over—carried a kind of intimacy. They made her feel special. Courted, like she was some kind of noblewoman in a regency romance and he was a rakish explorer.

The letters, it turned out, were just one part of Sean's aggressively analog life. He frequently forgot to charge his phone and insisted on wearing a watch—not even a good watch; Carrie had bought him a nice Panerai with a leather band for their first anniversary, and he'd kept it in a box, insisting he'd lose it or break it if he ever wore it, certain that she would have never forgiven him for leaving a nice watch on the side of a cliff somewhere by mistake. No, he had a cheap, utilitarian wrist watch and wrote in leather-bound journals and, from time to time, took puffs of sweet-floral blue smoke from a pipe as he sat on the porch in the evening. Not often. He wouldn't dare sacrifice his lungs, put his precious climbing career at risk—but once in a while, for the aesthetic, sneaking away like a kid with a forbidden treat.

All habits that had at first attracted her, intrigued her. She'd been fascinated by this lanky, anachronistic man with his head in the clouds.

Then they'd become things that annoyed her, drove her crazy over time. His obsession with this old-fashioned persona, the identity he cultivated rather than ever being real or authentic with her. Childish affectations that seemed with each passing year to become more like personal insults, something he was doing at her just to get under her skin.

Things she had badgered him to change.

Things she didn't realize she'd miss until it was too late.

In her tent each night, Carrie glances around surreptitiously as if certain that someone might be watching, even though she's the only one inside. Then she eases the leatherbound journal open and runs her fingertips lightly over the inked pages, breathing in the scent of sweat that permeates the cover. Sean smell. The last piece of him left to her in the world. She holds it dear and reads each page a half-dozen times before turning it, wanting to memorize every word and deeply, superstitiously afraid of reaching the end.

Because she knows: there will be a moment when the writing stops.

She knows it's impossible for him to have chronicled his death—he would not have had it with him when he died, or how else would Maya have come to have it?—simply knowing that the entries will stop is enough to keep her from venturing too fast and too far into the book.

When she reaches the end, Sean will die a second time. A final time. And she cannot bear the thought.

CHAPTER TEN

Sean's travel diary, dated April 29

We lost a member of our expedition today.

It feels strange writing about it, disrespectful, but I feel like writing it all out is the only way I might be able to purge the event from my mind. As it is, every time I close my eyes I see him fall. The image is seared permanently into my brain. I'm afraid I'll have nightmares about it tonight, maybe every night. I've seen climbing accidents before, but never anything like this. I've never watched someone die right in front of me like that.

His name was Ang Dawa, one of the Sherpas in our climbing crew. I had never really spoken with him. Maya speaks reasonably good English, but most of the other Sherpas in our group keep to themselves. Regardless, from the limited time I spent with him, Ang seemed like a good man.

A strong climber, too. He worked without complaint and did his job well. I don't know if he had any family he left behind, or what he did in the off-season. I should ask Maya whether she knows. Not, I suppose, that it makes any difference now.

I don't know how much of this journal might end up published, either for *Summit Fever* or in a memoir. This isn't the story I ever wanted to be writing, but it feels like an important one to document. In case it ever becomes important to publish this climbing journal where laypeople can read it, let me explain what happened in the simplest way I can.

Traditionally, on an expedition like this, Sherpas climb ahead of the team to set fixed ropes and prepare the path for the rest of the climbers. On other expeditions, this job might be done by the strongest or most experienced climbers themselves, but Everest draws an unusually high number of amateurs with little in the way of technical skill.

So the Sherpas set up routes to make the path to the summit as safe and simple to navigate as possible. Climbing the mountain requires so much endurance and carries so much risk already, between the altitude and the sheer size of the endeavor, that having experienced Sherpas set the ropes is one way to cut down on the risk for everyone. My group is small, and Warren and Susanne are hardly expert climbers.

This is Susanne's first major peak. All the more reason to set the ropes well in advance of the climb.

I volunteered to go ahead with the Sherpa team to help set the ropes. I figured that since I have some experience, it's the least I could do to help. And I've been eager to make some progress toward the peak, after so much time waiting idle at Base Camp. Truthfully, I was greedy for a look at more of the mountain. Every day camping in the peak's shadow, it's been like the mountain was whispering to me, inviting me to come closer.

One of the most dangerous parts of the whole Everest journey is also one of the closest to Base Camp. The Khumbu Icefall is a frozen stretch of glacier and crevasse that must be crossed to get onto the path toward the peak. Thick boulders of ice are scattered over the path, and climbing over them is exhausting work. Towering glacier walls groan and creak as you pass; they are constantly moving and shifting, quietly shoving their way down the mountain. Sometimes, enormous chunks fall off to create deadly avalanches. An avalanche in the Khumbu Icefall was the single greatest disaster in modern Everest's history, and the risks rise every year thanks to the warmer springs and glacial melting.

To cross the Icefall, you must set up a series of ropes and ladders. The ropes are there to clip onto so that if you slip, your tether will catch you before you fall. The ladders are laid like suspension bridges over the split chasms that open in the ice. Between the ropes and the ladders, traversing the Icefall becomes fairly straightforward—but laying down this infrastructure is perilous, and crossing the rickety ladder bridges isn't easy either. It's less of a risk for climbers, who will only need to navigate the Icefall once. But porters carrying gear up the mountain might need to traverse back and forth over these same ropes multiple times per expedition. The danger to them is so great that they've begun using helicopters to carry the gear up instead, skipping the Icefall. But that plan, too, is perilous. The air is thin up here, and helicopters have a bad habit of dropping out of the sky when there's not enough atmosphere. And the helicopters can disrupt the delicate balance of the ice, worsening the avalanche risk.

Damned if you do, damned if you don't.

But I'm stalling, burning paper. It's so much easier and more soothing to write about these details and explanations than it is to revisit what happened today. But for Ang, and perhaps for my own mental peace, I'll do my best to record the events while they're fresh, before they have a chance to be twisted by nightmares.

Maya didn't come with us to set the ropes. She was back at the camp with the other clients, tending to whatever business needed to be dealt with at camp. It was just me and a small group of Sherpas, some from our group, some from others. Communication was broken around me—they mostly preferred to chat with each other, and more or less ignore me—but I could follow along well enough with what needed to be done.

We had been working at it for about half an hour when it happened. Despite the chatter around me, an unearthly, eerie calm descended on the Icefall. The air held the same hushed and muted feeling as the first night of proper winter, when the snowfall insulates the sky and dampens sound. Here in this frozen and treacherous wonderland, a graveyard hush cut through by the deep moans of the ice straining against its own weight. Every minute in the Icefall, I worried about an avalanche. The serac rumbled like a giant, sleeping beast, and I held my breath and prayed against the fear of a thousand pounds of ice breaking free.

Caught as I was in this concern, I didn't immediately notice when Ang fell. He was some way ahead of me, setting the screw-like pitons into the ice that would hold the ladder steady. I don't know what happened; maybe the screw slipped its hold in the ice, or maybe he overbalanced reaching beyond his grasp and failed to hook himself in place. But by the time I looked up, he was beginning to fall.

The cry was what alerted me. Nervous as I was about the threat of avalanche, my senses were tuned to every possible sound. Ang's startled yelp, however muffled by his gear and the distance between us, seemed almost deafening. I lifted my head from my own work and saw as his body thrust forward, arms pin-wheeling for balance.

My hand dropped to my hip, where the safety rope linking us together was letting out slack—too quickly, far too quickly. Before I could think, I grabbed it with both hands, the rope burning through my gloves as it rushed through it. I staggered forward, almost pulled with the force of it, and I threw myself backward, grabbing the climbing axe clipped to my belt and flinging it into the ice, its teeth digging deep as I caught myself from tumbling after Ang.

But the rope that should have held him, the rope that should have anchored us together, was loose. Ripped from its anchor on either side, like it had never been secured at all. I watched its end whip in the air as it broke free from the spool at my hip, fluttering toward terrible freedom. How did two pitons break at once? How could the rope rip away so quickly? It was like Ang was being thrown, like some invisible thing had plucked the lifelines and tossed him away like a toy, a puppet with its strings all cut.

He seemed to fall in slow motion, taunting me in my inactivity. I was frozen, maybe a dozen feet from him, forced to watch as he hurtled down. A crevasse lay beneath him, a chasm several feet wide and impossibly deep. It could not have taken him more than a second to fall, but the moment seemed to stretch on forever, like he was tumbling through water rather than air. My body tensed with the urge to lunge for him, to try to catch him, but my grip held firm to the axe, survival instinct that almost certainly saved my life. I watched as he tumbled down into the ice.

A sickening thud resonated up from the crack in the ice. I leaned forward to peer down into the crevasse. By this time, several others of the crew had rushed forward as well to offer assistance—all of us, too little, too late. Ang lay below, his body caught up in loose ropes like a fly in a spiderweb. He was very still. His body had tumbled against the sharp icy face of the crevasse and caught in a narrow space, suspended from a ledge. From here, easily twenty feet overhead, I could make out the dark spread of blood where his head had been cracked open on the ice. His mouth was open, lips pulled back in a grimace, and that ghastly smile would look up at us from the crevasse for an eternity. His eyes, wide open, stared blankly upward, the whites catching the light. He could see nothing, but he stared at me all the same, his stare boring deep into me.

When I close my eyes, that's the sight I see: his wide, staring eyes and his grimacing, toothy death smile.

Knowing it was too late to save him, we tried to retrieve his body anyway. It was too far to reach, and the ropes he carried had gone untethered, following him into the crevasse. There was no way to bring him back, and no way to nudge him deeper down the crevasse without sending someone down to do it—a dangerous endeavor, and to what purpose?

We would have to leave him there, his body lying broken upon the crimson-stained ice, and accept that he would leer up at us with that awful rictus grin each time anyone crossed the Icefall, until the mountain itself decided to shift its ice and swallow his body whole.

CHAPTER ELEVEN

Carrie awakens to Tom leaning in close over her sleeping bag. His body crowds the tent, bulky with thermal gear. In the darkness, she cannot properly see his face, and a thrill of fear shoots through her, reflexive, primal. She scoots backward. Her body tangles in the sleeping bag, threatens to strangle, to enclose, and her heart strains against her ribs like a trapped creature.

It's momentary, this spike of panic, swiftly replaced by understanding of where she is. Who she's with. Why the ache and chill has settled so deep in her bones. Why breathing feels like sucking air through a straw.

She runs a hand back over her hair, smoothing the braid she's tied it in. Yawns, her body shuddering. Squints at the narrow sliver of sky visible through the tent flap. It's blue-black, and cut through with stars.

"I'm sorry if I startled you," Tom says.

"It's dark."

"I know. We're crossing the Khumbu Icefall today, and getting through it as fast and early as possible, before the sun is bright, is going to be a big deal. Sun means snow-blindness and glacier melt, and it's hard enough to get across the ice without that." He hesitates. A sheepish smile crosses his face as he catches her eye. Her gaze darts away, again peering at that dark patch of sky. "Sorry. If it's any consolation, you get an extra day to rest on the other side? But then the acclimatization trips start. That'll be a lot of work. Up, down, rest, up, down. Like that."

"I can't wait," Carrie replies, dryly, pawing through her belongings for warm outerwear to slide into before escaping the warm safety of the sleeping bag. Her bladder aches. She remembers with dismay that it will be a very long time be-fore she sees a real toilet again. Down here, it's all squatting over trenches. Higher up the slope, hanging from the side of steep cliffs, she doesn't even know. She hasn't thought to ask, and she's not looking forward to needing to.

But that's a matter for later.

Tom is a gentleman and looks away as she slithers from her sleeping bag, even though she's nearly fully dressed for warmth: unflattering thermal underwear, a double layer of socks and mittens. Bundled up like a baby against the cold. But she appreciates it all the same. By the time she returns to the campsite, bladder voided and a steaming cup of weak camp-stove coffee in her hands, the Sherpas are already disassembling the tent and getting provisions ready to haul to the next location. She watches them in the semi-dark, mesmerized by their speed and efficiency. Lopsang sees her watching and smiles, hefting his pack higher, and gives a thumbs-up. She returns the gesture, though she's feeling anything but confident.

She finishes the coffee and sits on a rock, struggling clumsily with the laces to her boots, clipping on the cleat-like crampons. Her fingers are blunted with cold and heavy gloves, but she manages to get everything locked in place on her own. Then she checks over the gear in her pack: ice axe, rope, carabiner, belay device. Today she'll be using the climbing harness that wraps around her hips like some kind of strange bondage gear, ropes and straps designed to keep her easily attached to a climbing line. She steps into it, double-checking the connecting straps, and tries not to think about what would happen if any part of the assemblage fails.

Overhead, the sky is clear and shockingly bright despite daylight being hours away. Far from city light pollution, the stars illuminate the sky, swirls of galaxies suspended in fog. Beneath their twinkling gaze, Carrie feels a sense of unreality, an unnerving certainty that she is not wholly present.

Exhaustion, she thinks dimly; nothing more than tiredness creating that surreal sensation of being not-quite solid.

Isn't it funny how altitude and tiredness and grief all affect the body in the same way?

The caffeine from Lopsang's weak-brewed coffee starts to kick in, tingling through her skin, and it does nothing to chase away the surreal, half-present sensation. Only drives little pinpricks through her skin, pattering through her guts like raindrops.

Tom comes to check on her, to see whether she's finished with her gear and double check all the clips and knots and attachments. He gives her a run-down of the plan, what to expect as they cross the Icefall. Most of it makes little sense, ringing against her tired ears. She absorbs what she can but lets the rest wash over her, so much background noise. It doesn't really matter. She'll be strapped in so snug that she might as well be a piece of cargo. She's being hauled up this mountain more than really climbing it, and sees no problem with that.

She'll never climb another mountain after this. She has no need or desire to master or even understand technique and good form. She needs to know only enough to survive a day at a time.

All the same, she's gathered the gist of Tom's instruction.

The Icefall will take hours to navigate. It will be dark and cold for most of that time, but traveling in the dark is necessary. Once the sun is up and warm, the ice will melt and shift. The Icefall is a living thing, a glacier in constant slow motion. Softened, melting, it will slide and shift and open chasms into a great yawning nothing beneath. The sun will reflect off the surface, bright and dazzling and blinding in its whiteness. Traveling in the small hours of morning will give the best chance of safety.

The Sherpas will need to cross back and forth over the Icefall several times, Tom tells her. But she only needs to make the journey once—twice, if they're counting the descent, but that's so far in the future it doesn't bear thinking about.

There will be dozens of aluminum ladders laid out like narrow bridges across crevasses or up the slopes of craggy glaciers, their tops hooked into the ice. There will be ropes laid out by the Sherpas who have already crossed, the climbing teams ahead of them on the journey to the summit. Carrie will be clipped into these ropes, tethered by her harness to the lifelines. She'll also be tied to Tom, whose body and knowledge will serve as the failsafe if anything goes wrong.

"I'll be right behind you," Tom finishes. He tries for a reassuring smile, extends a hand for her to get up. She hesitates before taking it. His grasp feels remote and foreign through the dual thicknesses of their gloves. "I'll keep an eye on you."

What he does not say hangs heavily between them: he had filled this position so many times for Sean, had been there as his failsafe on so many mountains. But not the time it counted.

What he also does not say: he would protect Carrie with his life precisely because he had so horribly failed with Sean.

They pack their bags, heaving heavy packs onto weary shoulders. Carrie eats an energy bar in three bites, mechanically chewing, not really tasting.

They start at last for the Icefall, shuffling over stony, icy earth, bent low under the weight of gear. With each step, she tries to remind herself why she's here—the mission that's brought her halfway across the world to this land of frozen stone. It's hard to remember in the cold and dark. A part of her yearns for the safety of Base Camp, its music and food and rowdiness.

She's tucked Sean's diary into her thermal underwear, the leather cover pressed close to the hollow beneath her breast. It feels warm there, like the touch of skin. She imagines it throbbing, a heartbeat that echoes her own unsteady pulse. Imagines that she's bringing Sean with her.

Come and find me, she can almost imagine it whispering against her skin. *You've come so far already. See it through.*

As promised, Tom follows behind her, ready to catch her if she falls. Maya is ahead, quiet and careful. She hasn't acknowledged Carrie's presence all day, and Carrie doesn't mind at all. Pemba and Lopsang trail behind the three of them by several paces, carrying the rest of their gear and supplies. They move this way—single-file, like a crowd of ants leaning low into the wind, identifiable only by the bobbing illumination of headlamps and the quiet crunch of spiked boots into the crust of ice—up the path from Base Camp, away from safety and toward the looming columns of ice that serve as barrier and gateway to the rest of the mountain.

The Icefall rises up around them, shadowy beyond the circle of light from their headlamps. Seen from above, it looks like a wide, flat path curving down the mountain's slope, showing its true nature: a river of solid ice, flowing from the peak at an agonizingly slow but inevitable pace.

But down within it, it looks neither flat nor calm. Ice and snow piles up in jagged steps and pillars, a pile of rubble deposited from millennia of glacial flow. Carrie sees its enormity only in pieces, peripheral glimpses of dark shapes, ice that sometimes catches and refracts the light. The ice sometimes glints and sparkles, reflecting the stars overhead.

She tries to keep her attention focused on the path ahead, concerns herself only with where to put each foot. Hand over hand on the ropes. Feet stepping into the tracks made by Maya ahead. There is comfort in deliberation; the effort chases away her other thoughts, fills the inside of her head with a pleasant white-noise hum.

She focuses on her breathing and the steady effort of every footstep, and on the feeling that Sean is with her, pressed in close against her body.

They travel this way a long while. She's not certain how long. Time is a liquid concept here, free of the constraints of clocks and deadlines. There is only the slow brightening of the sky, the stars crowded out by the gray haze of morning. Only the incessant burn of effort tearing through her muscles, a searing, buzzing ache that rips through her thighs and seizes the back of her calves. Only her breath, coming in jagged pants, the fog curling around her face and crusting in ice that freezes around her goggles.

No time. Only effort.

Foot here. Grab this. Eyes fixed on Maya's back, gaze focused on the wisps of black hair visible in loose strands beneath the tight cap and climbing helmet. She's peripherally aware of Tom behind her, the fog of his panting breaths. The solidness of his body waiting to catch her if she falls behind.

No one speaks. There's no need, and not enough air to waste on it. The threat of avalanche, too, keeps them silent. The glacier is precarious, a living thing, and vibrations could loosen the grip of snow on ice, break off chunks of frozen terrain.

The glaciers groan, waking from slumber in the darkness. The sun, still invisible below the horizon, calls out its morning alarm in the form of golden light peeking out from between parting clouds. The ice responds with a deep rumble, the earth itself yawning awake.

Something shifts, cracks. It sounds like a gunshot. An explosion of white powder, snow blowing in a thick haze, a chunk of ice and snow tumbling down the slope. It bounces, kicking up more ice in its wake, and suddenly they're climbing blind, thrust into a white-out.

Carrie's sense of calm and complete focus shatters, a dam breaking in her mind.

Her skin prickles, a full-body shudder racking through her from spine to limb. She nearly misses her footing on the ladder. Lurches forward, catching herself on the ropes. The line goes taut, Tom pulling on his safety lead. He makes a quiet, inarticulate noise behind her. But she does not fall. She shifts her weight, hands trembling, and finds safe purchase on the metal rung of the ladder. She feels her pulse in her throat, and the biting cold as she sucks a thick breath of air through her teeth.

The avalanche is over, the snow beginning to settle. Just a small one, then. Not enough to sweep them away, to bury them in snowy graves. But enough to remind them that it could.

Carrie blinks, clearing snow from her brow with the back of a gloved hand. The ladder is laid at an angle, anchored firmly into a chunk of ice on the other side. Beneath her, a crevasse opens wide and gaping. It's impossible to see to the bottom, but the light from her headlamp casts a broad circle over the icy maw. She stares, momentarily transfixed, before feeling an impatient tug on the rope. She lifts her head, sees Maya looking back at her, her face barely visible beneath her fur-lined hood.

Was this the place, Carrie wonders? She shifts her arms, tucking an elbow against her side to touch the diary without losing her hold on the safety line. Reassuring herself that it's still here. Feeling for the warmth, the echo of her heartbeat. Was this where Ang had fallen?

The journal, of course, does not answer.

The crevasse, silent and depthless, offers nothing.

Following Maya's lead but keeping her head down, eyes searching, Carrie finds herself unable to escape the curiosity of each glance downward each time they pass over a crevasse. Her attention fractures between watching for avalanches from above, and for the sight of a body below, its mouth split wide in an eternal grin.

The small team makes slow but steady progress. The sun makes a journey of its own, racing them to the summit. It gleams golden against the slope. Carrie's body aches with exertion, oxygen-starved muscles crying against the effort of every step.

In all, the journey takes them five hours. A shorter hike than the many days that brought them to this point, but deeply exhausting in a way nothing up to this moment has been. Impatient as she is to reach the Death Zone near the peak's summit, she's grateful knowing they'll soon be stopping, camping, taking days to recover from this singular burst of effort.

Still, she's not so exhausted to be unaware of her surroundings, and she's seen no bodies tucked away into icy graves. No glimpses of colorful down jackets or corpses caught on ledges.

Where is Ang?

Surely no one could have come for the body. A sense of betrayal gnaws at her as they reach the end of the path, stopping to rest and recover from the climb. Sean's diary is her only link to him, her only glimpse into his final days, a final arbiter of reality. She needs, desperately, to trust that it's telling the truth.

So where is the body? Where is the dead man left behind in the Icefall, as Sean described?

The terrain levels out on the far side of the Icefall, offering a relatively smooth path of slushy ice and gravel dotted with boulders. They stop there, on the path to Camp I, to eat and drink and catch their breath.

The camp is visible up ahead, a hint of jewel-bright tents fluttering in the wind. It will be well-populated by now, bearing climbers who got an earlier start at the ascent, and Sherpas who went ahead with ropes and gear. Other climbers will follow over the next few days, filling the vacancies left by those who went ahead, a brief but frenetic churn of bodies, waves crashing against the shore of Everest's stony slope.

A deep tiredness has settled in Carrie's limbs. Crossing the ladders and clipping into the ropes, her body felt animated by a humming electricity, but that wire now seems to have been cut. Everything feels unbearably heavy. It's like concrete has been poured into all of her joints, thick and sludgy and pooling into the crevice of every limb. She can imagine it hardening, fixing her into place, a statue at the exit to the Icefall erected like some kind of monument. A cautionary tale.

She cannot imagine ever crossing over it again.

She's not even entirely sure she'll be able to get up again now that she's dared to stop.

She wiggles her toes inside her boots, just to remind herself that she can. She holds a thermos cup in two hands, sipping cautiously lest she lose her trembling grip.

"You did great out there," Tom says, smiling. He's half-perched on a nearby boulder, his pack nestled into the snow at his feet. He bends over double, circling his knees with his arms, stretching his lower back. When he looks up again, his face is red and puffy. He's pushed his goggles up atop his head, and they've left faint trace-marks around his eyes, like some comically wide-eyed owl.

The Sherpas move past them. Pemba flops to the ground, leaning against his heavy pack like a backrest. He tilts his head toward the meager warmth of the risen sun and closes his eyes. Lopsang exchanges low words with Maya. Carrie can't make out whether it's English or not, and allows it to fade into white noise as she pins her attention on Tom instead.

"Is this the only route?"

"What?"

"The way we came. Is this the only way through the ice?"

"No. Not at all." He glances over his shoulder. The sun has transformed the path they had journeyed in darkness into something unrecognizable, made alien by the changing quality of light. "There really is no one route through the Icefall. It changes all the time for safety. The glacier itself changes, too, always moving around. Why?"

She shakes her head, avoiding his gaze. She looks past him to the mouth of the pathway, the ice glinting like diamonds under the sun. "Nothing. Just ... something I read in Sean's diary."

Tom's gaze flicks away, almost embarrassed, like he's been caught staring. His mouth forms a hard, thin line, expression gone stony, and Carrie can't begin to guess at what's going through his mind.

Before she can puzzle it out, Maya and Lopsang circle back to them. Maya extends a hand for Carrie, heaving her to her feet.

"Do not stop too long," the Sherpa advises. "Your muscles will seize. The cold settles in, you will not want to keep going. Wait until camp. Then you can relax."

Carrie's legs quiver under her weight, knees threatening to buckle, but she manages to hold herself up as Maya pulls away. She shuffles one heavy foot forward, too tired to lift it. Marvels at the knowledge that, somehow, she will have to climb the rest of this mountain.

"Maya ... " she takes a few more steps, awkwardly keeping pace with the Sherpa as the others fall into step behind them. "Do you ... I mean, did you—know someone named Ang?"

The guide glances sideways, a cool smirk crossing her lips, dark eyes glittering. "I know many Ang. But you mean the dead man."

Carrie's heart strains in her chest. "Yes. From Sean's climb. What happened to him?"

"He died."

"The body," she presses, knowing that Maya is having a go at her, that those glittering dark eyes contain laughter. "Where is the body?"

Maya shrugs. Looks like she might say more, but keeps her gaze fixed ahead instead. Watches the path, silent, leaving room for Carrie's thoughts to amplify.

Tom catches up, panting slightly. He's spooling loose climbing line in a loop between mittened hands as he walks, tightening what had been Carrie's leash. What will be her tether once more, when they embark again on a trickier slope. "What's up? What's bothering you?"

A frustrated noise catches in her throat. "It's nothing. Just. Something I read in Sean's journal. A Sherpa who died. I thought … his body should have been visible. When we crossed the Icefall. I looked for it, but it's gone."

An odd look crosses Tom's face. He slides the circle of rope over his shoulder, tucking it into his armpit. "Bodies disappear sometimes."

The words catch her off guard, and icy clench of fear grasps at her gut. She hefts her pack, busies herself with her gloves and the hem of her down jacket. Turns away and fixes her eyes on the ground ahead, those last trudging steps to camp.

"I mean. People find them, and do what they can to put them to rest. Cover them with blankets or nudge them down into a crevasse." A moment's pause, like he isn't sure whether to continue. "Have you ever heard of Green Boots?"

She shakes her head, not daring to look up.

"Over on the Tibet side of the mountain, there's … this sounds so fucked up. But. Okay. A man died near this cave in the Death Zone, close to the summit. Just sort of laid down right by the path. Everyone knew him by the boots he was wearing."

"Everyone?"

"Other climbers. He was there for years. You … you couldn't climb the summit without passing his body. It was like … a landmark, I guess."

Carrie lengthens her stride, ignoring the searing cry in her muscles. "They used a dead body as a mile marker?"

"Something like that. Like I said, it sounds kind of fucked up when you say it out loud." He falls silent a moment, just the sound of his breathing and the crunch of his boots on snow, then catches his breath enough to keep talking. "Anyway. Green Boots went missing. Someone moved the body off the trail, I think. But then people have reported seeing it still—where it had been, or in some other place. Maybe they're confused. Maybe an avalanche moved the body. I have no idea."

"Ang," she says, finally, gripping to the mystery with tenacity that barely makes sense even to herself. "The Sherpa who died. No one could have moved his body. It was unreachable. Down in a crevasse. That's why … why they had to leave him. It said. Sean said."

Her hand moves, fingertips touching the space beneath her breast where the journal lies, tucked against her heart.

"The mountain," Maya calls back to them, "takes what it wants. Who it wants. Now—enough wasting breath. We're nearly there."

Camp I has a very different energy from Base Camp.

Carrie feels it immediately as they enter the crescent of tents. She makes her way to the freshly erected mess tent for a chance at a proper rest and a hot meal, courtesy of the Sherpas—not her own Pemba and Lopsang, but those working with other climbing groups, the porters and guides who came ahead to fix ropes and set up the tents. Carrie doesn't question how the rations are divided or who decides which person gets to fight through the exhaustion and effort of the climb to start the camp stove and brew tea and soup broth. She merely accepts both gratefully, taking small warming sips so as not to turn her stomach into a hard, cramped stone.

She removes her crampons and boots and rubs out the hardened knots in her tendons. Probes at the calluses and tests each toe for frostbite. Changes out her wet, frozen socks for two pairs of fresh ones—inner pair and outer pair—and puts the boots back on. Her fingers feel swollen and clumsy, and she struggles with the laces, but she manages. Feels proud of herself, prouder than she should for something as simple as lacing boots.

There are no sightseers at Camp I. No selfie-taking families, no guitar-carrying musicians, no joints passed among

129

revelers. No casual vacationers take the risk of a climb through the Icefall. From here until the summit, there will be only those single-minded climbers with an eye toward the finish line.

There will be no more stray dogs circling the edges of camp looking for scraps. No more shaggy yaks hauling supplies. There are no animals at all at this altitude, as far as she can tell. No birdsong, no rustling undergrowth—or undergrowth of any kind, for that matter. No life.

Everything up here is either cold, unyielding stone and hard, crusted snow, or part of an attempt to conquer the same.

The only people between here and the summit are the dead.

Pemba and Lopsang join her for a while in the mess tent, drinking tea and chatting with Sherpas from other expeditions. They leave soon, though, to go pitch the tents. From here on, their expedition will have just two at each camp: one housing the three Sherpas, and one shared between Carrie and Tom. At each camp, a shared mess tent and shared gear and supply tent will be erected as well, the effort of putting it up, taking it down, and hauling it up the mountain spread among the porters.

"You're OK to go," Pemba says, catching up with Carrie later in the afternoon. Tom has found her, and the two of them are set up outside, enjoying the radiant warmth of the sun while it lasts. "But no fucking."

"Excuse me?" Carrie blinks, not sure whether she'd heard correctly.

Pemba grins, teasingly, and points to the tent she and Tom will be sharing. He lifts both gloved hands to make a rude pantomime, a finger thrusting into a cupped fist. "Fucking," he repeats with the relish of someone who has recently learned a new dirty word. As if that were the thing that needed clarification.

Carrie has never been one to blush. She tends to do it in reverse, skin going death-white as blood drains from her face, and she feels it now, the cold of receding color in her already pale cheeks. Her eyes go wide, too shocked to be angry. Too confused to reply.

"Very funny," Tom says, dryly. "You'd better be warning all the other expeditions, too."

Pemba just grins at him, giving a thumbs-up, and shuffles away to tend to something else.

As soon as he's gone, Carrie rounds on Tom. "Hey, what the fuck?"

"He's just messing with us. You know. Because of the tent situation."

Her heart is pounding. "Why would they think we were … ?"

"I'm sure they don't," he assures her swiftly, running a hand through his feathery hair. He offers an apologetic smile. "Not really. The Sherpas have a … superstition, I guess. Against having sex on their sacred mountain. It defiles it, see? Angers the goddess. So they get very … anxious."

She sucks air through her teeth. Holds it. Tries to calm the frightened bird that's overtaken her heart. *It's not about you. They don't even know you. They don't know anything about you.*

"Is that … a problem, up here? I mean. Are people actually … in the cold … ?"

"Danger does strange things to people. For, uh, some folks, the thrill of it can certainly … get the blood pumping." Tom was not a reverse-blusher. His cheeks flushed red, a crimson glow making its way up his neck and spreading in blotches along his jawline. "If it makes you uncomfortable, I can talk to Maya. See if she'll swap tents with me."

Carrie shakes her head quickly. "It's fine. It's not … a big deal." She doesn't want him to know it bothers her. Wants to shut down that line of thinking before he even has a chance to bring up what had happened between them once. What wouldn't, couldn't, happen again.

That night, and the nights that follow, reading Sean's diary becomes a covert act, as intimate and embarrassing as masturbation. She waits, listening for the sound of Tom's steady breathing before easing the leather covers open, sliding deep inside her sleeping bag with her flashlight to pore over the handwritten pages.

Hiking the Appalachian Trail was Sean's idea of a first date.

They had been corresponding for months at this point, Sean's hand-written letters arriving in increasingly thick envelopes as he poured himself onto the page for her. Carrie always feared her responses would be woefully inadequate, but he never seemed to mind.

To be certain, they met up a few times—quick coffee dates, shared dinners when his adventures brought him through her neighborhood and allowed them a chance to meet up. But the first real date had been in the mountains.

"I'm gonna need you to clear your schedule for me," Sean told her. "Give me a week and I'll change your whole world."

It was a ridiculous idea. People didn't just drop everything to go hiking in the wilderness with some guy they knew almost entirely through letters. That's how people got murdered.

What if he turned out to be a psycho?

What if she got all the way out there and realized she didn't really like him as much as she thought? She'd be stranded in the wilderness with a guy she didn't want to be with, and no way to get away without counting on him. Absolute madness.

She did it anyway.

Or maybe she did it because it was a bad idea. Because Sean—old-fashioned, gentlemanly Sean, with his letters and his journals and his adventuring—was exactly the right kind of dangerous.

So the summer between graduation and law school, Carrie had packed her bags and flown out to Tennessee to meet Sean at the trailhead.

"We won't be hiking far." He grinned, rearranging the constellation of freckles over his perpetually sun-chapped face. "It takes months to do the whole thing. I won't make you commit to anything like that. Just a little teaser."

He knew first-hand how long the trail took. He'd done a through-hike, all 2,200 miles of it, backpacking through small towns and pitching his tent in the wilderness, going feral for half a year to complete the journey the year he graduated high school.

"I just put on a pack and some hiking boots and started walking," he'd explained to her, almost sheepish, modesty too self-conscious to be anything but sincere. "I didn't give too much thought to where I was going or why I wanted to do it. I just knew I didn't want to be home anymore. I wanted to see a new thing every day, be someplace new every night. So that's what I did."

"You're insane," Carrie told him, and laughed, intoxicated by his madness. "How much did that cost you? How did you manage, like, food? And everything else?"

They were lying snuggled together in a tent they'd pitched together off the trail. Beneath them, the Smoky Mountains were holding true to their name, heavily obscured by rolling fog. It was damp and chilly outside, but inside the tent, warmed by the tangle of their bodies, was snug and cozy.

They were not making good time on the trail. In part because Carrie was an inexperienced hiker. In larger part because they had not succeeded in keeping their hands off each other for long. Far from meeting him in the mountains to discover she didn't like him as much as she thought, Carrie's week in the Smokies revealed that she liked him significantly more than she'd imagined. She liked his big, knotted hands and the strength and sureness with which they touched her body. She liked his long, muscular legs and the way they tangled with hers.

"It wasn't that bad," Sean replied, his fingertips brushing the top of her pants, probing questioningly beneath the waistband of her jeans. "I had a car. I sold it, because I wouldn't need it, and that kept me fine. Then I got home and sold an article about it to a climbing and outdoors magazine. 'High school graduate tackles Appalachian Trail alone' was a pretty splashy pitch, it earned out okay. And that's … y'know. History. How I got started, I guess."

He smelled like sweat and pine needles and she scooted back close to his chest, pressing as tightly into his grasp as she could, like she wanted to melt into his warmth. Lose herself in his body. "You're amazing."

He kissed the nape of her neck. "So it's working?"

"What?"

"My clever ruse. My scheme to make you fall in love with mountain-climbing."

"You're making me fall in love with something, Sean Miller, and I don't know if it's the mountains."

CHAPTER TWELVE

Sean's travel diary, dated May 5

My dreams since the incident in the falls have been jumbled, anxious. Like going to bed with a fever. It's like my brain is consumed by the sight of Ang's body. I'm exhausted, but sleep remains elusive, even though I know it's essential to my own survival on the mountain. I don't know whether I'm coming down with some illness, or if my body, already pushed to a point of strain from the brutal elements of the mountain, is reeling from the emotional shock of witnessing such a gruesome death, of coming so close to touching it myself. I am not naive. I have seen and endured climbing injuries before. But something about this is different. Maybe because, however many times I go over it in my mind, I can't make sense of how Ang fell. What snapped the ropes loose? What invisible force hurled him faster than gravity into that narrow chasm of ice?

I'm distracting myself by writing in this journal, hoping that if I pour enough of the terror out onto the page, I'll make room at last in my mind for sleep. It doesn't seem to be working. I am hyper-aware of the sounds of the mountain, the creaks and groans of its shifting ice. In the darkness, half-dead with exhaustion, I swear I can hear things whispering outside, just beyond the tent. I do not know whether the voices come from my own mind, or from the darkness that spreads around us.

There's something else strange, too. A sense that time is slipping around me. Maybe because we've lost so many of the electronics, all those creature comforts. It feels like we've moved backward in history, hardly better off than Mallory and Irvine in the way we huddle in the cold. I shouldn't be writing like this. I should be resting. I don't want to talk to anyone, not the other climbers and definitely not Maya Sherpa. But I want to get this out of my head.

When I close my eyes, I see his face. That awful grimace, teeth bared like some blank-eyed animal, the red-black blood pooling and freezing fast to the shelf of ice that would become his tomb. The only safety from the vision is to open my eyes, but he's here with me in the darkness as well, lingering just outside of the glow of my electric lantern. The batteries will wear down at this rate, and I will be left with nothing against the night, but I cannot bear to shut it off.

In the circle of darkness beyond the lantern's glow, I have seen something moving. Something that prowls outside of my tent, casting a shadow against the illuminated vinyl wall. It walks on all fours, spindle-legged and knobby-kneed, and I know that if the light goes out, nothing will keep it away.

I don't know whether I've been awake or dreaming when I've seen this. The time is all blurred together.

I want to crawl out of my tent and go talk to someone, speak with Maya or one of the climbers, just to hear a human voice and know for sure one way or another whether I'm dreaming or hallucinating or awake. But I'm afraid to open the tent flap. I'm afraid to crawl out into the darkness and meet that spindle-legged shadow head-on.

I feel like I have not slept in days. I feel like this night has worn on forever.

All I can do is sit up in the lamp light and write, busying my hands and my mind.

Maybe I'll write myself a bedtime story. When I come down this mountain and edit these notes and journal entries together into something useful, maybe I'll see this story and have a laugh at what a superstitious, fever-brained coward I'm being tonight.

When I was a kid, after I'd gotten my first taste of travel stories, I became obsessed with Mallory and Irvine and their doomed summit bid in 1924. I imagine everyone who has thought seriously about climbing Everest must have done the same at some point. It's an amazing story, one of the greatest and most enduring mysteries in the history of mountaineering: two men, heeding the siren's call of adventure, making three attempts at the impossible only to disappear tantalizingly close to their unreachable goal. A body that was never recovered, and with it, a camera that might hold the evidence of their success or failure, and quite possibly a record of what actually happened in their final moments.

A mystery left unsolved, and made unsolvable by time.

As a kid, I ate it up. I think all children have a taste for the macabre, and I certainly did. The exploits of long-dead men in far-away places served as a good escape from my far more mundane reality, rife as it was with the horrors of a father who drank too much and a mother who had long since learned to stifle her complaints.

Regardless, there is one story of the ascent that haunts me now, circling around and around again in my memory, a small detail that keeps surfacing like the solution to a problem dangling just out of reach, like a forgotten word just at the tip of the tongue.

Mallory and Irvine's expedition began their ascent from the Tibetan side of the mountain, the opposite slope from where I am now camped. As they made their trek upward toward what would eventually become the north face's base camp, the crew stopped at a monastery in the shadow of the peak. There they received shelter and a meal and a piece of advice that none of them yielded: turn back.

The people who lived and worshiped in the Himalayas had never thought to climb the peak. The mountain was a mother goddess, an immutable fact of the landscape, both sacred and terrible. To climb further would be an act of rebellion or defilement. It would send climbers into a god's world, a place where man was not meant to travel, and in my mind these monks must have been both horrified and confused by the desire of these white foreigners to do this impossible and pointless thing.

But Mallory's party continued up the slope, of course, ignoring the warnings. And in true mythic fashion, they would be beset by tragedy the whole while—weather that seemed to conspire against their progress, the disappearance of the explorers themselves. One could be forgiven for thinking the whole thing to be a cursed affair. The mountain, getting a taste of human sacrifice, was perhaps awakened rather than sated.

I think about this tonight in my tent, rather than thinking about Ang and the way he died in front of me, though both amount to the same thing.

Every moment of my life feels as though it's worked toward this event. Every step I have taken, from discovering children's books with glossy pages showing photographs of mountains, to my time in the wilds that cradled me and protected me from the darkness at home, to the breathless peaks of North America, South America, Asia. Everything I have ever done has brought me to this place, and the idea of turning back now is laughably implausible.

It's not just about the story that I owe to *Summit Fever*, although my bridges with them would be irretrievably burned if I don't deliver it, and I might owe them back advances that I have no way of repaying.

It's not even about my own desires and ambitions toward the peak, not really.

Because if I'm being honest with myself, right now, hunkered down in my tent, shivering with the type of cold that soaks through flesh and permeates into bone, I do not want to climb this mountain.

I have not slept properly in days, not between the nightmares and the thinning atmosphere and the pervasive exhaustion. Days—and the journey to the summit is still impossibly far away, many more weeks of climbing and camping and waiting. There will be no reprieve; the air will only get thinner, my muscles wearier. I want nothing more right now than to be at home in bed, cradling my wife and sleeping a comfortable and dreamless sleep far away from the staring eyes of corpses.

But at the same time, I know—with the same unshakable certainty as a natural law, like my certainty in the existence of gravity—that I will not leave this mountain until I have reached its peak.

I cannot. The goddess has seen me, and she will not allow me to leave until I have done my part.

CHAPTER THIRTEEN

The broad hollow that cradles Camp I is known, officially, as the Western Cwm—a Welsh word, pronounced inexplicably like 'coom,' a holdover from Mallory's time. If the Sherpas have their own name for it, Carrie doesn't know. She doesn't think to ask.

It's strange being on this mountain, part of a group but feeling so apart from it. She does not belong here. Not on this mountain, and not with these people. Not with the other climbing expeditions, with their excitement for reaching the summit. And not with her own small crew, this assemblage of strangers—and Tom, who had always been Sean's friend first, who is linked to her now primarily by the thread of grief and a past she has come to lay to rest.

Other climbers can tell at a glance that she's green, and they seem to avoid her. Not that there's much socializing at this altitude—expeditions seem more likely to keep to themselves, only conversing to discuss matters of safety and logistics, everyone keyed up and anxious to get further up the slope now they've reached this first crucial milestone. She catches a rare smile or dip of the head in greeting as she moves around camp, but no one lingers long to chat. They can see her newness, her inexperience, in the stiff brightness of her freshly bought gear. In the raw pinkness of her wind-chapped skin, which has never endured such lasting exposure to the elements.

Maybe they think she is a liability. They don't want to get close so they don't have to feel compelled to rescue her when she gets herself into trouble.

Or maybe they are turned away by the pervasive miasma of sadness that clings to her, repellent in its misery.

As a lawyer, she's well-acquainted with impostor syndrome. She's approached every day at the firm with a quiet, buzzing background worry that she's actually a fraud, underqualified and overconfident, that someone will find her out and expose her. But now that worry is thrown into harsh perspective.

She is a good lawyer, whatever her self-doubt tells her. She is experienced and educated and skilled.

But she does not belong on this mountain.

In that she is, truly, a fraud.

"Why do you climb?" Maya asks her one day as Carrie sits and tries to stretch her tight, sore muscles after returning from the first acclimatization trip. Up the slope, down the slope, a day of rest—repeated once or twice, until Tom is certain she's ready. The dance that makes the mountain climb excruciatingly long, and which is skipped under penalty of altitude sickness, psychosis, death.

A miserable, exhausting and necessary evil.

"You know why I'm here," Carrie replies irritably. She's out of breath and aching down to her bones, and she does not like the way Maya's beetle-black eyes crawl over her, probing and insightful with their unspoken judgments. "I'm looking for my husband."

Maya shakes her head. "If you only wanted a body, you would pay others. Sherpa would climb for you. Find a body, cut it from ice, haul down the mountain for you. You have the money. We do this thing, always there is someone wanting to pay us for this. But you don't do that. You fly here yourself, insist on climbing yourself. Why?"

"Because ... " she hesitates. A flippant response dances on her tongue, but she bites it back. It's a fair question. It deserves an answer, whether or not she wants to give it to Maya.

She could certainly have paid for a Sherpa team to do a search-and-recover for her, to excavate the body and haul it down the mountain, even to ship it back to the U.S. It might have been cheaper, and it certainly would have been safer.

But it wouldn't have been the same.

She did not want to sit in the safety of her home in Chicago, waiting by a telephone for news from the other side of the world. She did not want to lie awake each night and wonder whether they had found the body. She did not want the agony of hearing that he had been found, only to be crushed with disappointment if the body itself could not be retrieved. What would they have done? Taken a snapshot? Was she supposed to grieve over a blurry photograph? How could she ever really believe that this awful thing was real if she never had the chance to see it for herself?

"Sean loved the mountains," she feels herself saying, her mouth moving and forming the words before she realizes that they're true. "He loved climbing so much more than I have ever loved anything in my entire life, except maybe for him. And before I can grieve, before I can have a chance to heal, I need to understand why."

She blinks, surprised at the strength and clarity of this response. As if the truth has been dredged up from deep down, excavated from some dark and muddy place inside of her. She chances to meet Maya's eyes, searching for a mirror of the surprise that she's feeling.

But Maya merely nods, a satisfied smile touching her lips. As if she expected nothing less than the deepest, rawest truth. As if people often come to this mountain to speak their truths. And perhaps they do. Maybe Maya has listened to several such confessions, and asked only to hear Carrie make this offering here. Maybe in the cold and silence and bone-weary exhaustion of the mountain, where survival is calculated on the minute, there simply is no space for bull-shit. Perhaps the mountain demands honesty because it is a sacred place. All those stories of desperate men on quests, climbing to the apex of mountains to ask a question of wise men, ancient yogis who understand the nature of the world—perhaps the wise men are not the point. Were never the point. Maybe the climbing itself, the mountain itself, is the vehicle of truth.

Or maybe Carrie is reading into the Sherpa's silence the things she wants to hear.

There is a fatalism to the acclimatization trips. They are es-sential, a vital part of climbing. But they are also futile, spin-ning wheels in the face of progress. Climb up, climb down. Climb up, climb down. They trek the same route several times, Maya or Tom alternating in the lead, each time Carrie begging her body not to betray her at the higher altitude.

She worries that they will never move on from this place. That she will be caught in an endless, Sisyphean cycle. That Tom is trying to break her will, force her to give up on her journey through this agonizing battle of attrition.

But the others are doing it, too.

Other climbers, other expeditions, enduring the same miserable slog, building the same improbable stamina in the face of conditions humans are not meant to endure.

And so she stays quiet, and follows the rhythms each day, the cycles of exertion and rest.

Nothing could have prepared her for the excruciating boredom of mountain climbing. Hearing Sean talk, recounting his adventures, she had always imagined climbing as a deep thrill. The scope of it, the depth and breadth of stillness between the moments of exertion and danger, was lost on her. There was simply no way of understanding from the ground what it would really be like.

Sean had tried to explain.

"Thrill-seeking is jumping out of an airplane or driving too fast on the highway," he told her one night. "If you care about danger, mountain climbing is just going to waste your time."

Tom was in town, stopping by to visit, and the three of them were seated on the back porch, several beers deep between them. The night was warm, rich with cricket song and humidity, and it was hard to imagine any hardship or struggle in such a pleasant atmosphere.

"Rock-climbing, maybe," Tom suggested. He lifted his beer bottle by the neck, tilted it toward Sean.

"On a climbing wall, sure. I guess." His nose wrinkled. He was unconvinced. "Mountaineering is not about danger. It's about control. Mastery of something. Of technique, of yourself."

"Everything's about control with you," Carrie told him. She'd meant it teasingly, thinking of his fear of flying, his oft-repeated complaints about putting his life in the hands of pilots. But it came out harsh, heavy with hidden resentments.

"It's about submission, too, though," Tom said, quickly, eager to fill the awkward silence, to shuffle the conversation along and away from danger. "Knowing that everything is so much bigger than you. The mountain is bigger. Your team is bigger. You're not important. You're not anything."

"Cheers to that," Sean agreed.

"Submission and control," Carrie said, shaking her head. She heard a sneer in her voice that she didn't mean, didn't want, but couldn't contain. "You boys talk about the mountain like you're fucking it. Like it's a mistress." Quietly, then, half-muttered, "A mistress would probably take up less of your time."

The atmosphere shifted and soured. Went cold, despite the warm summer night air.

Tom chuckled, nervously, opened his mouth, about to try for a joke or a change or topic, but Sean cut him off. His voice was low and calm.

"You don't have to be jealous, Carrie. You could come with me."

"Thanks, but one of us has to have a real job." Carrie wished he'd yell. Wished he'd snap at her, so she could feel justified in snapping back—could validate the anger bubbling up suddenly and unexpectedly in her chest. There was no stopping it. "I work like a grown-up so you can go off on adventures and pretend like I could just drop everything to go chasing after you!"

"You knew who I was from day one." Wounded. Hollow. Not a drop of anger, just a pained resignation, and she wanted so badly for him to scream at her. "I'm sorry if you thought that would change."

Tom looked between them, an awkward interloper caught in the vise-grip of the feud, and it was his panicky gaze that drove Carrie away from the patio table. She was drunker than she thought; she felt the booze make a complete circuit through her body when she stood, a woozy head rush sending her spinning.

"Never mind. Forget I said anything." She brushed past them. Miscalculated the distance, bumping the table, hard. The corner nipped at her hip. It would bruise, and she'd awaken in the morning with an ache there, forgetting where it had come from. "You two have fun without me. It's what you're best at. I'm going to bed."

She fumbled with the latch on the patio door and made her way down the hall, trembling by the time she reached the bed. Every nerve was singing with anger. Her head spun.

When Sean came to bed not long later, she pretended to be asleep. She let him pull in behind her, wrapping his arms around her waist. Felt him smooth the hair back from her forehead and kiss the hollow between her neck and shoulder. "I'm sorry," he whispered against her hair.

She should have returned the apology. That time, and the other times when they came back to the old fight, chased it round and round in hopeless circles. Should have apologized, too, when he called from Lukla to let her know he'd landed, that he'd try to stay in touch from the satellite phones on the mountain but he couldn't make any promises. She should have apologized instead of saying, "Don't worry about it. We'll talk when you come home."

And now it's too late. Now any apologies will be to his corpse, if she's lucky enough to find it.

At least she has his diary, but it's approaching its end. There are pitifully few marked pages left, and she's afraid to read them. The blank pages at the end of the notebook are a miserable reminder of the lost opportunities, a future they wouldn't have. In those pages live their future children. The trips they'd planned. Nights on the patio, listening to the sounds of the city, a glass of wine or bottle of beer beading condensation as they talked.

Apologies unspoken, amends unmade.

Facing those blank pages, knowing what they mean, forces her to slow her pace through the remaining entries. There won't be much time for reading when they leave Camp I. The climb will only get harder from here, more arduous and exhausting. But she'll stretch the entries as far as they can take her.

She's not ready to let him go, not a second time, a final time.

CHAPTER FOURTEEN

Sean's travel diary, dated May 10

Something is with me on the mountain.

I have felt that way intermittently since Ang's death. I had thought, then, that it was merely a nightmare, some guilt-fueled hallucination or the precursor to some sort of sickness. But weeks have passed since. Has it been weeks? It's difficult to keep track of time here. I don't even know if the dates are right anymore, or if I'm missing days. It's harder to tell without all the electronics, though we wouldn't have many with us by now anyway. We would have left them by now. Here, we've brought only the few supplies that are essential to our survival. And this journal. Which I fear I may soon be unable to write in.

We have all become thin and ragged with the effort of climbing. The body is not meant to survive at this altitude.

It begins to eat itself, auto-cannibalism in an effort to fuel its vital processes. Sleeping is difficult when there is so little oxygen available. Under the stress of exertion and the poor sleep, it's hard to get much food to stay down. Warren has been sick these last few days. I hear him at night, clawing his way through the snow outside his tent to relieve himself away from where we sleep and not always getting far. The camp reeks, a stench dampened only by the pervasive cold.

Days start in the darkness of night here, climbing toward the twilight of dawn with our headlamps guiding the way. Ang is dead. Maya has not spoken more than a few words to me in days; I fear she may never speak to me again. I don't know whether I have enough information to write the feature *Summit Fever* sent me here to complete.

But I am getting distracted.

The important thing is that I am not alone on this mountain. And I don't mean my fellow climbers. Not my small guided expedition, and not the others who are preparing to summit with us—the documentary crew with their heavy cameras, the foreigners whose language provides an inexplicable but somehow comforting undercurrent of white noise against the silence of the high camp.

There is something else.

I first noticed it weeks ago—has it really been weeks?—the feeling of someone or something prowling around beyond the tent. I was certain it was a nightmare.

But I am wide awake now. Waking and sleeping, it's there all the time now. It follows me when I step outside, when I move around the camp, when I venture out onto the path. I feel it, too, in my tent at night, lurking just outside. If I am quiet, I can almost hear its heavy breathing.

That's the strangest thing about the high camps of Everest. You have never heard anything so silent. No traffic. No bird song. Not even the shrill of insects. Nothing is alive here. There is only sky and stone and snow. In the evenings, you can lie awake in your tent and hear the breathing of the people in tents all around you, the quiet hiss of oxygen delivered through masks, the soft rustle of sleeping bags.

But this sound is something else. It is a deeper breathing, as if filling massive lungs. No human has ever breathed like that.

The mountain makes its own noises, also. The creeping and groaning of the settling ice. The song made by gusts of wind blowing past weathered slopes. And a deeper sound, almost imperceptible, the low moan of ancient earth settling and spreading in repose—like the settling of an old house, ratcheted up to an impossible scale.

I have not been sleeping well. In the darkness I have a lot of time to listen to these sounds, and to wonder at the certainty that something is watching me.

I wait and listen for its voice. I expect it to whisper to me, the way it did on the slope when I was following Maya, when it urged me to jump.

The others do not speak of it, but I'm sure they can feel it too.

When it passes like a shadow beyond the edge of camp, unseen, the Sherpas fall silent. I have seen Maya tilt her head as if listening to instructions or trying to catch a soft voice on the wind. Even if my fellow climbers don't seem to notice, the Sherpas know. I know I am not going crazy.

Altitude psychosis. That's what they call it, when you return to the real world, the place where life still has a foothold and the stories of the mountain no longer make sense. But I think maybe they call it that because you can't understand what the mountain is like, not really, unless you're on it. It plays by its own rules. This is an alien landscape, a part of the universe as uncanny as the depths of the ocean or the vast reaches of space, and it is hubris to think we understand any of what goes on up here. We may climb the mountain, but we do not conquer it—not its slopes and not its secrets.

I'm in my tent now, writing by flashlight. I shouldn't be. I should be conserving my batteries. But I am afraid of the darkness. I am afraid that if I shut off the light, the thing that prowls beyond the camp will come closer. The only way I can justify leaving the light on is to write, and so I am, my fingers forming words as if my life depends on it, and maybe it does. I don't know if any of this will make sense. Perhaps when I come back down the mountain, I will read back over this and think about altitude psychosis and realize how silly I was being.

I want to think that.

But I cannot believe it is true.

The batteries are dying. They won't hold power. The light has begun to flicker. I don't have much time. It will be dark here soon.

The thing outside is coming closer.

I can hear it breathing. The smell is coming through the tent, a rancid hot stench like rotting meat curdling through the vinyl walls.

I will not look. I can see its shadow in the periphery but I will not look at it. It can smell me. It can see me, see through me. I feel its eyes on me. But I will not look.

Maybe it will go away.

CHAPTER FIFTEEN

The Cwm is surprisingly warm, well-protected as it is from the wind by the high mountain walls guarding its valley, warmed by the radiant sun glistening off snow in every direction.

The day before they're due to start their final, real trek to Camp II—no more turning back, no more acclimatization—Carrie finds herself in a patch of sunshine, face upturned to the sky. It's almost pleasant. Almost springlike. Maybe it's just the acclimatization finally taking hold, her body no longer struggling simply to survive at altitude, her stomach no longer twisting in irritable knots around each meal, her fingers no longer tingling from perpetual cold and low oxygen.

She's perched on a boulder, back pressed against another upright stone. Sean's diary is open in her lap. She's wearing only a light jacket over her thermals, and the freedom from the oppressive thickness of her usual down coat and layered clothing gives her a feeling almost of weightlessness.

She closes her eyes and allows herself a moment to appreciate the environment. There is no birdsong or trees or traffic. Only a soft whisper of wind, the deep low grumbling of ice and stone shifting and resettling, the living glacier of the mountainside slowly reshaping itself. Noise from other climbers: boots crunching over snow, tents rustling, metal cups and utensils clinking.

With her eyes squeezed shut, Carrie pretends that the weight of the journal in her lap is Sean's hand, lightly resting on her thigh. His head in her lap, her fingers tangled in his messy red curls. Tries to remember how it felt, to have him close. How he smelled. How he tasted.

He's slipping away from her, his memories overwritten piece by piece by the scrawl of his handwriting, the texture of soft leather.

"Does it help?"

The voice cuts through her imaginings, and Carrie opens her eyes with a slow, nearly drugged blink, as if rousing herself from sleep. "What?"

Maya gestures to the diary. "I see you with it, always. Whenever we are not climbing. Does it help you?"

An uneasy smile. It's become hers so deeply—become a part of her—that she has forgotten that it hasn't always been hers. That she has this tenuous link back to Sean now only because Maya gave it to her. "Yes. Thank you."

A silent pause. Maya's dark eyes watching her curiously. An air of anticipation stands between them, as if each is expecting the other to say something.

Just as the silence is beginning to stretch into discomfort, just as Carrie's starting to feel the awkward weight of it settling in, Maya speaks.

"Are you ready?"

"For Camp II?"

"For finding him. For looking." Maya nods toward the journal. "It goes quickly from here. We make the trip up and back, up and back, for weeks now. But Camp II will be a day or two. Camp III, the same. And then … "

"The Death Zone," Carrie finishes, and her gut goes cold. All the warmth and good cheer from the pleasant weather leaks out of her at once. There is only a twisted, uneasy feeling, mingled dread and excitement.

Maya nods. "The Death Zone," she agrees. A slight smile twists at one corner of her mouth.

"Where Sean was … " Carrie trails off. Swallows. "You were the last person to see him, weren't you?"

Maya shrugs. "I saw him on the way to summit. He got well ahead of the group. I was behind, helping the others. But your husband was eager. Always go, go."

Carrie averts her eyes, squirming under the intensity of Maya's gaze. The sky is the wrong shade of blue, the color skewed by the thinness of the atmosphere. "He didn't have a Sherpa with him?"

"You asked about the dead man, Ang. We were down a man, after. Your husband could have hired another Sherpa at a different camp, but he would not do it. He did not use a Sherpa after Ang. He carried his own gear, set his own ropes."

Of course. She should have realized it as soon as she read it in his journal, as soon as she caught herself looking for the body in the crevasse. Ang would have been his personal Sherpa. Sean would have felt guilty. Responsible. He would not have wanted to put anyone else at risk after what happened.

Anyone, that was, but himself.

The journey between Camps I and II is such a familiar path by now that Carrie completes it nearly on autopilot. Not every acclimatization trip has brought them this far. Some have gone along other paths, or only partway up the slope.

But she's been here twice before, and this third and final trek to this new milestone is going smoothly.

The area between the camps is called The Valley of Silence, Carrie learns. It should perhaps be called The Valley of Murmurs instead; aside from the sounds of climbers walking single-file ahead and behind, the swish of fabric and the panting of breaths, there is a lower, deeper sound. A quiet rumble, the ice creaking and groaning beneath them.

The slope is gentle, the path worn wide and broad and smooth like a giant riverbed. It looks like something that should be easily traversed, but Tom warns her to stay clipped in, to hold to the ropes laid out like a lifeline over the surface of the snow.

"Underneath all this snow is pure glacier," he explains. "It cracks and shifts. A crevasse could open up right beneath us."

She imagines the mountain as a giant, slumbering creature, one whose body is covered in mouths that yawn open at intervals to swallow whatever traverses its form. Can almost feel the beast breathing, the faintest of undulations underfoot with each step forward.

But it's not the mountain. It's her pounding heart. Her trembling limbs.

Excitement singing through her body—excitement and terror and that awful, twisted sort of hope.

Despite the acclimatization, the progress she's made, she is still desperately, agonizingly out of breath by the second half of the five-hour climb.

She'd been a smoker for a brief period in college, when it was fashionable to play with mortality by pretending that it didn't mean anything. She'd never really liked it. She didn't like the way it smelled, and she didn't like the sticky, gummy feeling at the back of her throat and lungs when she woke in the morning. And her occasional, social smoking habit broke off completely after being with Sean.

He didn't force her to quit. Never even mentioned it directly. But he opened up a part of his life to her, a part she struggled to share, and she knew she'd have to leave the cigarettes behind if she had any hope of joining him. After their week together on the Appalachian Trail, she never picked up another pack.

But she still suffered, that knife-point stabbing in her lungs an aching reminder that she had not been training as long as he had. That she was not made for this the way he seemed to be.

After the Smoky Mountains, they'd fallen into that honeymoon phase where everything is new and lovers are gentle with each other—all questioning touches and probing questions. He took her on hikes and camping trips every time she could get a weekend away. In the winter, when camping seemed unpalatable, he scheduled dates at the university's indoor climbing wall. She learned on her own that following him where he wanted to go meant surrendering some parts of herself: the parts that smoked, that over-indulged in weekend box wine, that preferred to sleep in a comfortable bed late on a Saturday morning.

These were non-essential parts that must be shed and discarded like so much excess baggage if she wanted to keep up with him—because Sean was gentle, but he never waited up.

So, she quit smoking well before they were married, before she found her footing at the law firm. Years past, now, and still her lungs ache with the distant memory of waking with a tight chest, a dry, hacking cough to clear some invisible obstruction. She takes in air in shallow sips and has to force herself to remember to breathe deep. Getting enough air feels like drinking a thick milkshake through a straw.

They are only nearing 21,000 feet. The oxygen tanks won't be used until the final leg, the stretch in and near the Death Zone. They have not packed enough oxygen to waste any on this lower elevation, not if she wants to spend time wandering free of the established trails and search for Sean's body.

So she will not ask for the oxygen. Tries not to let Tom see, either, that she's struggling. It's nothing. Just nerves.

Just an hour or two more, and they can rest for the night. Maybe two. Then up and over the Lhotse Wall to Camp III, then on to Camp IV, the final leg. The Death Zone—and just beyond, the summit.

Summit.

She catches herself thinking of it in those terms, and the consideration actually stops her in her tracks, brain stuttering over itself. She feels the insistent tug of the short rope linking her to Lopsang ahead of her. Tom, trying and failing to pull up short behind her, bumps into her. Steadies himself with his hands on her shoulders.

"Okay, Carrie?" he breathes into her ear, a blast of warmth that immediately freezes against her cheek.

She nods mutely, not finding the excess air to speak. She's grateful for the excuse, because she does not know how to otherwise explain the hesitation, how to make sense of the mental processes that have stuttered to a halt.

Summit?

Where had that thought come from?

She is not here to reach the summit. That is not what she paid money for, not why she traveled to the far side of the world. Reaching the top of a mountain is a meaningless achievement, an empty accolade that had stolen the life of her husband, stolen the life they would have had together.

She is here to find Sean's body, to lay it to rest, to close the door on her memories and find peace enough to move on.

So why is she thinking of her journey in terms of camps and summits?

From the Valley, the summit is still only a vague concept. From here, she can see sheer white granite walls and icy glaciers. Patches of cold blue sky. If the mountain were the slumbering beast she imagines, the summit would be its head—held low and hidden, only to emerge once awakened.

Summit.

The word plants itself like a foreign object embedded in her consciousness, and she forcibly shoves it from her thoughts as she presses forward, once more bending double against the effort of the single-file trudge through the snow. She feels the movement of the line, the tether to Lopsang and Pemba and Maya ahead and Tom behind, always Tom, leashed to her like a loyal dog.

She does not need to be clipped in, she thinks, suddenly resentful. Others are climbing this stretch of mountain without ropes. It barely even qualifies as climbing, this part. Just hiking. One foot in front of the other. No need for an axe, no need really even for crampons.

Her hand drops to the carabiner at her waist. Thumb fumbles for the latch. She'll unclip. Break free of this ant column, just to prove that she can.

Summit.

The word echoes tauntingly in her mind. It does not sound like the voice of her own thoughts. It sounds like someone else, a voice she does not recognize. But it's familiar, too, somehow. Like something that's always been there, whispering to her, waiting for her to be able to hear.

Like Sean, she realizes, and a shudder seizes through her body, muscles locking into place with the force of it. Her hand drops away from the carabiner. Her fingers are numb, useless. Like something Sean said in his diary.

She stutters once more to a halt and Tom again bumps into her. He says something, but she doesn't understand, or doesn't hear. Then the tension is going out of the rope and he's steering her to sit down. He's fussing with his pack, pulling out tea from a thermos and looking worriedly down at her, worse than a concerned mother looming over a feverish child.

"Carrie? You okay?" He grasps her hand, fingers curling awkwardly around hers, navigating the extra thickness of the gloves. He slides the thermos into her hands and cups both of his around both of hers, like she needs to be taught how to hold a cup. Like he doesn't trust her not to drop it.

He ducks his head, gaze seeking hers. His eyes peek out over the gaiter that protects his face, looking sharp and bright and so full of concern that she has to fight an urge to slap him.

She imagines splashing the tea in his face. Imagines screaming at him: *You're not the one I love. You never were. Stop being nice to me. Stop acting like things were different.*

But the urge passes as swiftly as it came. It settles down into the darker place inside her, perhaps curling and coiling its nasty serpentine body around whatever voice had been whispering 'summit' into her ear.

"M'fine," she mumbles.

"How are you feeling?" He's still crouched down in front of her, his down-stuffed pants bunched absurdly, his body as bundled and puffy as a flightless bird. His hands have not moved from hers. "Headache? Nausea? Do you feel like you might throw up?"

His thumb strokes at the back of her glove, an idle gesture she doubts he even realizes he's making. The 'whish, whish' sound of fabric-on-fabric sets her teeth on edge.

"I know what nausea means," she manages, and is disappointed to sound more tired than irritable. She does not have the strength to take her hands from Tom's. She endures, with awful childish helplessness, as he lifts her hands in his to bring the thermos up to her mouth. She only just manages to nudge him away in time to drink under her own power, and even then, tea—not scalding hot after all, barely warm now—escapes the corners of her mouth, dribbles down her chin.

"If you need to go back—"

"I'm not sick," she protests, wiping at the excess tea with a sleeve. Thrusts the thermos back into his hands. Her skin prickles beneath her collar. Like something's crawling underneath, earthworms surfacing in a rainstorm. Every pore feels alive and suddenly she realizes she's hot, so hot, soaked through with sweat.

How can she be so hot, surrounded by all this snow?

"Problem?" Maya has circled back from the head of the group and stands over them now, arms crossed, brows lifted.

"No problem," Carrie says. "We're almost there. Let's go."

Her teeth click together, her jaw convulsing, and she clamps down hard to stop them from chattering. A shudder rolls through her body, and that doesn't make any sense because she's so hot. So stiflingly hot. She paws at her gloves, trying to get them off.

Tom and Maya exchange a look.

Tom grabs Carrie's hand, stopping her clumsy attempt to undo the Velcro at the wrist. Squeezes. Pulls. Maya takes the other, helping to heave Carrie to her feet.

Carrie's body feels heavier than it should be, like it's been filled with molten lead. Like all of it's drained to her feet and cemented her in place. She doesn't know how she'll shuffle two steps forward to get back in line, much less the hour or more still ahead of her.

But she'll do it anyway, because doing the impossible is what people come to this godforsaken mountain to do, right?

The voice in the back of her mind, with its alien familiarity, has fallen silent.

CHAPTER SIXTEEN

Sean's travel diary, dated May 16

I feel like I'm bungling the notes for this project. I don't know what I'm going to have available to write that feature article. I don't even know if anything in this log will make sense when I look back over it. But at this point, I need to write these things down somewhere because I can't talk about them out loud. The rest of my group would think I've lost my mind. They might even try to make me turn back around. That's how crazy it feels like I'm going. I look back at the other entries and don't remember writing half of them. I think it's better if I just don't read back over any of this until later.

(Maybe I should turn back. Maybe I should tell someone how I'm feeling. But for what? I'm not giving up this summit push because I'm scared of the dark. I might never get another chance. I won't be scared by ghosts of my own invention).

Anyway, a strange thing happened today.

I don't have an explanation for it. The likeliest thing is that my oxygen was simply malfunctioning, leaving me starved for air. At this altitude, it's hard to trust your perceptions. Your senses will lie to you. All the same, what happened was so bizarre, and so unlikely, that I don't know how to begin with understanding. I'm hoping I can make more sense of it if I write it out. Maybe when I read over this later I'll piece the details together in a way that makes sense.

So, yesterday. We were making an acclimatization trip between Camps III and IV, one of the final climbs between us and the summit push. According to Maya, we should be ready to make for the summit within days. She says we're doing well. One of the best groups she's guided. She says she's impressed with how well everyone is keeping up, even though only one of us has much professional climbing experience. Whenever she says that, she always looks at me like she's daring me to say something, like she's expecting me to argue, but she's right. Warren and Susanne are doing just fine. Better than me, honestly, unless they're going crazy up here and hiding it better.

We traveled, as we usually do on these acclimatization trips, at a distance from one another. The climbing isn't hard in this stretch, and being strapped in on a close rope causes more problems than it would solve. Between the blinding sun reflecting from the ice and the blowing snow, visibility can be difficult, and crowding raises too much risk of losing your footing or tripping over someone or getting tangled. There are stretches of the climb we've made where the path was already heavily crowded with other climbers, so any opportunity we get to spread out is always welcome.

But this means that, for long stretches, I climbed without knowing who was ahead or behind me. I only knew where I was putting my feet.

At one point, Maya approached me. She seemed concerned that I was not making good enough speed. She beckoned for me to follow, encouraging me to pick up my pace as we started back down the mountain path. I did not see any of the others, and that seemed strange, but then I had not bumped into one of my fellow climbers for some time and imagined perhaps we were going down ahead of them, or else I had somehow fallen significantly behind without realizing.

The descent seemed to take a very long time, however.

My body, already being challenged at altitude, protested against the additional stress of this unexpected exertion. My mind was beginning to cloud, that fuzzy feeling that accompanies drunkenness or long sleepless hours. I was grateful to have Maya just ahead, guiding me down the path, as I doubted I would have been able to find safe footing on my own.

However—and this is where my recollection becomes strange—I soon lost sight of her. A gust of wind broke against the slope, blowing gritty snow and ice across my field of vision. Maya, ahead of me, was little more than a dark shadow, a faint outline visible beyond the foggy expanse of blowing snow.

I removed my mask and goggles in an attempt to clear the ice. When I replaced my gear, the wind had died down, and Maya was gone.

I called out to her, but my voice felt choked. I was afraid to make too much noise for fear of an avalanche. They are less likely here, where the ground is more frozen and the ice is less volatile, but I would rather avoid taking a chance. All the same, I felt an odd awareness that, even if I wished, I would not be able to raise my voice. Like when you're in a dream and try to call out but can only whisper. I cannot explain it, but I was certain that the mountain itself had stolen my voice, suppressed it to maintain the level of ghostly hush that now filled the cold slope.

"Maya?" I remember rasping out, several times, and pushing my way forward, following the path she must have taken. All the same, I did not see her, and this puzzled me. It's difficult to lose sight of someone entirely on the mountain. I worried that she might have slipped, tumbling down the steep slope on either side, or else fallen into a wide chasm, a freshly opened crevasse.

But I saw no signs to indicate that anything like that had happened. Nothing at all seemed out of place.

Most unnerving of all, I realized as I trudged forward along the path we had chosen: there were no fresh tracks in the snow.

Snow on a mountain like Everest is hard, a firm crust that has built up over lifetimes. It is not easily displaced. Still, the spikes of our crampons do break through the outer crust, and there should have been some indication of that in the path ahead of me. There should have been tracks from other climbers, and there certainly should have been tracks from Maya herself.

I looked behind me and saw my own footprints. They were clearly made by a faltering and shuffling gait, but they still documented the path of my boots in the snow.

I stopped there, confused.

Had I somehow strayed from the path? Had I gotten turned around somehow, disoriented in the blowing snow?

Ahead, something seemed to move, a flash of color—deep blue. Had Maya been wearing a blue jacket? I could not remember.

But I followed it, climbing laboriously over the unsteady ground before finding myself, abruptly, at the edge of the world.

The slope broke away ahead of me, just feet from where I stood. I took two steps back and crouched on my heels on a broad stretch of solid, hard-packed snow, panting. A stride ahead, the mountain ended entirely, a sheer cliff that faded down into white nothing. Once the dizzy spell passed, I crept to the edge, peering down, seeking out that flash of color that had led me here. I expected to see Maya lying down below, tangled in a web of ropes like Ang, a grimace splitting her features, limbs twisted and broken at all angles, dead eyes staring up.

The thought sent a shiver through me, a paralyzing cold, and for a moment I did see it: the fan of her dark hair, large dark eyes staring blankly upward, a white gash of a mouth filled with teeth.

But as quickly as I had seen it, the vision was gone. There was nothing there.

"Jump," a voice said, just behind me, and I whirled around to look but could see no one. There was only silence and the gentle gusting of wind brushing against the slope.

"Fall forward. It would be so easy. Lean forward into nothing. Become part of the mountain."

The words in my ear this time, soft but clear.

I could not tell if the voice came from inside of me or some outside, unseen force. I knew only that its hold over me was strong. For a brief moment, I leaned forward, feeling the exhilarating weightlessness as resistance broke away; I felt like a bird preparing to take flight.

Then, realizing what I was doing, I wheeled my arms, struggling to regain balance. I threw myself backward, away from the ledge, and fell heavily, my tail bone screaming its protest against the hard crust of snow as I landed. I sat there, panting, trembling with cold and weakness and nerves, and was not certain for a long time whether I would be able to stand I was shaking so hard.

I did, however, eventually find my feet. The trembling subsided enough that I could walk.

The voice, wherever it had come from, did not return. I turned from the cliff, following my footprints, trudging until I found a place where the snow was more tightly packed by shuffling steps; there were many prints here, scattered messes caused by crampons digging deep into the snow, and I realized I had found the real path back down to camp.

By the time I returned to Camp III, I was more deeply tired than I have ever been.

My body protested its treatment. Every tissue ached, and I struggled to move one leg in front of the other. The sky, too, looked strange as I made my way into camp. The light was all wrong, the sun at an unexpected angle; it cast a strange, filtered light over the stones and snow, a surreal glow that rendered everything flat, more like a photograph than reality.

"Sean!"

Someone called to me, and they needed to repeat my name several times before I was able to recognize that the words were meant for me, or to put an identity to them. I turned, hazy, to see Warren looking at me with concern. I didn't recognize him right away. I stared, and must have had a very stupid expression on my face as I tried to recall everything I knew about this man I had been climbing alongside for months. His name was Richard Warren. He was from Texas. This was his first major climbing expedition. He was a doctor, now retired. A hobbyist pilot in his spare time.

I blinked several times, feeling like something had settled back into place, as if a part of my mind had floated away like a balloon but had at last been tugged down and tethered back into my mind. I felt like I was coming back to myself.

"Sean, are you okay?"

Warren guided me to sit down, brought me warm tea and sat next to me, his expression deeply concerned. As I began to sip my tea and recover, he explained what had happened when I got separated from the group.

I had been gone, it turns out, for several hours. They had discussed mounting a rescue to go back onto the mountain and look for me. They presumed I must have wandered off the path and gotten lost, disoriented in the blowing snow. Everyone had feared I might be dead. There was a group of Sherpas and climbers from another expedition that had been assembled for this purpose, only to see me strolling calmly back into camp hours after my apparent disappearance.

"That's not possible," I said, as he told me this story. "Maya was with me. Is she back yet? She can vouch for ..."

I trailed off, seeing Warren's expression—a skeptical frown that he tried quickly to replace with a smile, humoring me.

I related to him what had happened: Maya leading me, losing sight of her on the path, eventually finding the cliff to realize I had gone too far and needed to turn around. I did not mention the voice that had whispered to me on the mountainside. It seemed irrelevant now I was safe and warm. It also seemed like it would just suggest that none of what I'd said was trustworthy.

"I'll grant you that I got lost," I said, finally, "but she was definitely there. I could not have been gone more than an hour."

Warren's frown deepened. "Sean … that's. That's not possible." He gestured vaguely toward the tents. "Maya has been here for hours. She was the first back to camp. She's been here waiting for people to return. You can go talk to her about it if you're not sure, but I swear to you … there's no way you ran into her when you're saying you did. Your timeline doesn't make any sense."

I thought about the way she had disappeared into the blowing snow.

I thought about the unbroken, trackless path I had followed to the cliff.

I thought, too, of that voice at the side of the mountain, and of my momentary gripping certainty that the mountain had stolen my voice, that I would see her body lying broken among the stones. That feeling of settling back into my own mind, of being pulled away but tethered back to myself.

"The altitude does funny things to you, I guess," I said at last, trying for a self-deprecating smile.

Warren eyed me uncertainly, but finally shrugged, punching my shoulder amiably. "Well. Good to have you back. We thought we'd lost you there for a bit." He rose to go, then hesitated, giving me another funny look. "Get some rest, Sean. You're … not looking so good."

I was relieved that he didn't push the issue. I feared that, as a former physician, he might try to diagnose me with some sort of altitude sickness, might insist that I go back to a lower elevation to consult with a doctor—a suggestion that could cost me my summit bid. I feel fine. I will not sacrifice my chance at reaching the top over something so minor and inconsequential.

If I am a bit paler than normal, or sweating more profusely, then it's nothing to worry over. It has been a long and strange day, but I am sure there is a straightforward explanation for it all.

CHAPTER SEVENTEEN

Carrie awakens to the sound of a helicopter.

She's grown accustomed to the silence of the mountain, punctuated only by the sounds of other climbers—Tom and the Sherpas, the ships-in-the-night passage of other expeditions passing them on the trail or rustling in tents nearby. She is accustomed now, too, to the sounds of the mountain itself: the low moan and creak of shifting glacier, the faint whisper of wind over ice.

She's grown familiar with these noises the way she got used to the house she and Sean moved into together as newlyweds. At first, every creak and pop and groan made her eyes snap wide open. The house settling on its foundation, or the furnace switching on, or the ice maker hissing as it filled with water were enough to set her nerves on edge. But with time, she got used to the house and its rhythms, as predictable and easily ignored as her own heartbeat.

The mountain feels like that now.

The low rumble of voices, many speaking in languages she does not understand. The hiss of radio static from communication between groups—Sherpas higher on the mountain, ground control back at Base Camp, guides at lower camps. She can identify Pemba and Lopsang by their good-natured bickering, the tenor and pitch of arguments whose words she cannot understand. She hears, too, the hum of wind against nylon when gusts sweep over tents. The low, deep growl of ice shifting and cracking and settling in slow motion.

But the helicopter is a jarring addition, loud and invasive. The thump-thump-thump of the blades cuts through thin air and sets her teeth on edge, pressure mounting in her head as it flies over. She staggers from her tent to peer out and see what's happening.

Camp II sits near the base of the most intense climbing stretch they'll encounter until the peak. The stones and ice of the valley give way to harsh cliffs and treacherous terrain. Not that Carrie has seen much of it yet. After their arrival, she has slept nearly two full days, waking only intermittently, hibernating through some of the deep exhaustion that settled through her. She has a vague recollection of Tom fussing over her, of being asked questions, of responding through a tired haze.

But she feels fine now—fine enough to be irritated at the sound of the helicopter, at least.

It hovers overhead, stirring up stones and snow, flinging mountain debris in all directions. It makes tight circles, the pilot likely looking for somewhere safe to land amid the un-inviting slush and sharp stones. Carrie squints against the grit and crouches near her tent. Lifts an arm to block her eyes from shrapnel.

"Someone got sick," Tom explains, coming in behind her. He lays a hand in the hollow between her shoulder blades so as not to startle her, leaning in to breathe words against her ear so he doesn't have to shout over the chopper. His voice is hoarse, worn raw by the cold. "Up on the path. Climbing to Camp III, probably. They've spent all morning getting him back this far. My radio's been going nuts about it."

She doesn't turn to look at him. Her eyes stay fixed in-stead on the tentative hovering of the aircraft as it gingerly attempts to land on a patch of reasonably flat ground be-tween looming boulders. Sure enough, now Tom's said it, she notices the obvious detail she'd previously missed: a group huddled around a brightly-wrapped figure, a person rolled up like a burrito in a makeshift stretcher. She can just make out a snatch of blue, the jewel-bright jacket a spot of color against the gritty white and gray of the mountainside.

"What happened to him?"

Tom shrugs. "Cerebral edema, maybe. Or pulmonary. Hard to say for sure. I've just been picking up bits and pieces over the radio, nobody seems real clear on the details."

Cerebral edema is something Carrie is familiar enough with. It had been explained to her when Sean failed to return from the mountain—one of many theories given for how a seemingly healthy and strong climber could simply die for no reason. The brain, addled somehow by the thin atmosphere and lack of oxygen, would swell, fluid building up inside the skull. Without being surrounded by pressurized oxygen and removed quickly from the mountain, the victim would suffer psychosis, coma, death. Their eyes would bulge as their brain swelled to fill all the available space inside the skull.

A senseless, random, awful way to die.

Carrie can all too easily imagine Sean's face like that. His eyes wide and round, bulging from his head. His freckled skin pulled taut over a face misshapen by excess fluid.

What color was Sean's climbing jacket? Had it been blue? She can't remember. Tries to picture it in her mind and realizes she can't; another piece of Sean's memory dropping away, her brain purging details.

She blinks, forcing the image from her mind. Focuses instead on the helicopter.

"I didn't know they could get a chopper up here."

"Oh. Yeah." Tom shrugs. "I wouldn't say it's a common thing, but every so often." He gestures toward the crowd with his chin, indicating the wrapped-up victim. "I imagine they're some important who's-who. Someone with money. Rules always tend to bend when you can pay."

The helicopter has managed to land at last, and now people are swarming like a spilled-over anthill to get the blue-jacket man inside.

"This is about as far up as a chopper will go," Tom continues. He scratches thoughtfully at his face, where patchy stubble has begun to grow in. He looks strange with facial hair, and it seems as uncomfortable on his face as he does with its intrusion. Sean had always looked natural with a beard, wild and shaggy like a feral creature. Tom just looks unkempt. "Air above this point is too thin, and the slope's too steep. Landing that thing and taking back off is a gamble this high up. There's wreckage of a chopper up here someplace that crashed on a failed rescue. Nobody can get it down."

That, too, matches what she's heard before. The inaccessibility of the mountain's highest reaches was one reason frequently trotted out by sensible people for why Sean's body could never be returned home. Even if it were found—and everyone had been so sure to remind her, over and over, how hard that would be—it would be frozen solid. It would be heavy and cumbersome and possibly frozen into the rock itself. A macabre part of the landscape. It would have to be excavated like a fossil from the mountain and carried down by hand because no helicopter could land in the Death Zone to retrieve it.

It. He. Sean.

"But the helicopter can land here," Carrie says aloud, making conversation more with the voices in her head than Tom beside her.

"Yeah. It can." He hesitates. "And hopefully, for their sake, it gets off the ground again."

The swarm of people has begun to fall back. The blades are rotating again, picking up speed, tossing grit and gravel once more over the camp. Carrie squints away from it and finds Tom's chest, his body angling to shield her from the bulk of it. He wraps an arm around her shoulder, using an elbow to deflect the grit.

Even through the puffy layers of fabric, his coat and jacket and under-armor, she can hear the thump-thump of his heart. Can feel the pulse in his bony gloved wrist.

He pulls away, holding her at arm's length, suddenly shy about meeting her gaze.

"I'm glad to see you up and about," he tells her.

"Sorry. I'm all right. Just … tired."

A sad, hollow smile. "Rest up. Eat as much as you can these next couple days. Get the best sleep you can, too. From here on out it's going to get rough. There aren't many creature comforts at Camp III."

She peers around him, squinting up at the trail toward the summit—and the sheer white cliff face that needs to be navigated before they can stop. She can just barely make out the bright jewel tones of tents dotting the ridge, but when she blinks, the colors have shifted or vanished, replaced by glittering white. Perhaps she'd imagined it. Seen what she knew should be there.

"Got it." A hesitation. "Camp III. Then what?"

"We stay there for a bit. Rest up. Make sure all of the oxygen and gear works. It's all hard climbing between here and there, and I don't want to take any chances. And then it's just Camp IV. The Death Zone."

She nods, visualizing the route against the many maps she's studied in preparation. But no map can do this place justice. Nothing on television or the internet or in a book could begin to adequately describe this place—not its grandeur, or its spooky stillness, or the way it seems to whisper in the dark.

"Camp IV. And then Sean?"

"And then we look for Sean," Tom agrees, and cannot hide the weariness in his voice. "We'll work with Maya to get our best chance at figuring out where he might have gone. Could be anywhere between the summit and Camp IV. Hell, could even be between Camp III and IV."

He hesitates again, his gaze traveling up toward the peak, and Carrie waits for him to continue talking. When he doesn't, she nudges him. "Tom?"

"Sorry. It's just." He avoids meeting her gaze. "There have been hundreds of people on this mountain since then. That year, this year. Sherpas going up and back." He closes his eyes, a muscle in his jaw working hard against what he's trying to say. "Nobody's seen him, Carrie. You … you get that, right?"

She her body goes stiff, her mind resisting the words like a reluctant horse on a lead. She recognizes the truth in him, hears the sense, but refuses to acknowledge it. "He's here," she says instead, her voice low and flat. She edges away from Tom, starting toward the safe burrow of the tent. "He has to be."

This will be the last camp with a proper mess tent, Tom says, and their last night to have a proper meal. From here on out, and especially in the Death Zone, food will be reduced to candy bars and those questionable space protein gels that Tom keeps in his pack. There will be tea, but it won't really be warm. Nothing will be, not properly, until they are back down in the safety of the lower camps. The upper reaches of the mountain are not places of comfort. They are not places to linger, and there will be no comforts to make lingering more appealing.

He says this, more than once, with the conviction of a man certain he needs to make the point clear. As if Carrie has grown so attached to the mountain that she'll want to stay here forever.

"You have to promise me," he chides her for what feels like the hundredth time. "If we have to make multiple trips up and down to look all over the place until you feel satisfied, all right. Fine. But you're not staying up there more than a few hours. Half a day, tops. You're not spending a night near the summit, not on my watch."

The Death Zone is aptly named: a place so inhospitable that nothing can survive there. No plants, no animals, and certainly not the humans who climb through it with brazen disregard for the laws of nature. The atmosphere is so thin it contains just thirty percent of the oxygen found at sea level. The sky is dark, more black than blue at the edges. The peak yawns upward into space. The surface is as inhospitable as the moon.

Carrie does not intend to see the peak. She does not need to hear Tom's incessant warnings.

"Fine," she agrees, every time.

Summit, that quietly intrusive voice at the back of her mind adds, unbidden.

But tonight is their final hot meal, a last supper of sorts, and she settles into the mess tent—smaller than the one at Base Camp, cramped elbow-to-elbow, but big enough for her group and another expedition planning a summit bid in the upcoming days. That group is down two people from what they'd started with. One stayed behind at Camp II with some kind of burning fever and gut-chewing illness. The other was airlifted out of here—the blue parka guy whose sudden departure woke Carrie the day before.

What must it be like, she wonders, to get so far up the slope, to pay tens of thousands of dollars for gear and permits and guides, only to lose a summit bid to a stomach flu? How miserable would it be to fly home with your team, knowing that they succeeded where you'd failed thanks to dumb luck or the self-sabotage of a rebellious body?

Or even worse—what if the rest of the expedition didn't make it back? What if they died in a rock slide or were caught in a storm at the peak, dying one by one as they struggled to make it home, and the only person to survive was the one shitting his pants in a tent in the valley? What would it be like to come home and look a widow in the eye and tell her the real reason why you had lived and her husband died?

Her time on the mountain has, perhaps, made Carrie a little morbid.

Lopsang and another Sherpa that Carrie doesn't recognize—one of the porters from the other group—are cooking over a camp stove. She can barely smell it through wind-chafed sinuses, the cold dry wind robbing most of her senses of their edge. But what she can smell is pungent and spicy, little sensory daggers that burn. It is not entirely unpleasant. For once, her stomach doesn't turn at the idea of eating some intense foreign dish. When the alternative is a calorie-packed gel paste, she'll happily eat spiced lentils.

Well-fed, or as well-fed as any of them can be under these conditions, the small expeditions crowd together into a tent and turn to conversation. Carrie lingers on the fringe, finding no desire to join but realizing she craves the company, or at least the proximity of the company. How does she look, she wonders? Huddled in a corner, head inclined, skin chapped, hair knotted up in a messy bun. Does she still look like a delicate interloper, an outsider who does not belong here? Her normally pale forearms are darkened by sun and grime. She aches for the heat of a real shower, the steady thrum of hot water against skin. She longs for the comforts of a hotel, even the threadbare inn at Namche Bazaar.

Are the others thinking the same? Or is she still too weak and too green to belong here?

She learns details about the lives of strangers in small windows, snapshots that tell similar stories time and time again.

Here is a man who grew up with a love of mountains, worked his way through the Scouts, spent his adulthood bagging peaks and tallying achievements.

Here is a doctor who retired two years ago and found his life lacking meaning without a career to fill the empty hours.

Here is a woman who nearly died in a brutal car accident a decade ago and has spent every day of her life since recovery looking for new ways to live to the fullest.

So different, yet so similar, down in their core. Differing backstories, but a single uniting purpose: to summit Everest, to stand atop the world.

Everest, named by white men who thought they could tame it.

Everest, the mother goddess and economic backbone of a nation of diaspora.

Everest, who grows hungry at times, who demands sacrifice of those who dare to venture up its stony slope.

Ever-rest. It's like a cemetery name, a retirement home, all cheerful euphemism. *Where is your husband, Carrie? Oh, you know. Just up at Ever Rest, it has a beautiful view of the sunrise.* And then there'd be that quiet tut-tut, that false concern, because of course everyone knows what it means when you say that your loved one is at 'Shady Grove' or 'Sunset Meadows,' but it's the respectable way to talk about it because we dare not say dead, we dare not say buried.

Ever Rest, the world's highest cemetery, and she is here to visit the unmarked grave of a man she might have left, if the circumstances had been different.

She thought about it. In the months leading up to the summit push, she concocted a plan. He would return home, and she'd have sat him down for a good, hard talk. They would talk about deal breakers. They would have talked about her ambitions, and her inability to keep putting them on hold, and needing to know right now whether he was serious about them as a couple. If, now that he'd finally summited Everest, if he could at last put the mountains away and turn his focus to their life together.

If he could have said yes, they could have started to build something, finally.

And if not, well. Maybe she would have been done. Maybe she would have been divorced now, instead of widowed, and Sean would have been gone from her life but it would have been okay. Wouldn't it?

Because he's gone now, and it's unbearable. He's gone to a place so impossibly distant that she's flown across the world and climbed into the stratosphere to look for him, because she needs to know for certain that it's over. Because she knows that, somehow, this was her fault. Because she'd thought of leaving him when he got back. Because she had dreaded having that conversation.

Because, in a moment of weakness, she had thought about how much easier it would be if she never had to have that talk at all, if she could have been free without ever having to be the villain, the person who stood between her husband and the absurdity of his limitless ambition.

Because she'd thought of how much easier it would be if he never came home.

It was her fault, somehow, and now here she sits at the gates of Ever Rest Cemetery, the church doors of a graveyard situated on the body of a sacred mountain goddess, seeking penance or forgiveness euphemistically called closure.

"So, real talk," somebody is saying. A female voice—the car crash girl. "You've been up here before, right?"

The Sherpas who understand glance at each other, then nod, murmuring agreement. There is a time delay as others catch on, exchange quick words of understanding, then chime in. There is not a porter or guide who has not made this climb before. Most have been climbing since childhood.

Tom, too, nods, and so does another man—the Eagle Scout, a reedy bearded man who seems to be the leader of the other expedition.

"So all right. What's, like … the craziest shit you've ever seen up there?" She jabs a finger at the ceiling of the tent, but everyone knows she means the summit. The Death Zone.

Uneasy shifting, as if no one's sure whether to answer the question, or if it's even worth answering honestly.

"People do weird things when they're in trouble," Tom says, finally. He casts an apologetic look toward Carrie, though she cannot imagine why. "The altitude, hypothermia, snow blindness—all these problems get in there and mess with your head, right? So you see some weird things. I don't know. Like," he hesitates, and car-crash girl makes an encouraging noise, "people with hypothermia, some-

times they feel hot. I don't know why. There's some sci-
encey reason for it. But you come up the slope, sometimes
you run into some guy who's freezing to death but he's just
started tearing off his clothes. It's a pretty weird sight."

That leads to some rumble of amusement, something
loosening between the small group of experienced climbers.
They start opening up, then, exchanging mountaineering an-
ecdotes.

One had weathered out a storm on Denali by burrowing
into a rocky crag for three days, losing four toes in the pro-
cess.

One saw a man go tumbling from the sheer face of K2,
landing like a damp bag of cement on an icy ledge below.

All have suffered, in their own way, and all are proud of
it. Carrie stays silent and feels her expression draw pinched
and closed. Across the tent, she sees Maya huddled near the
thin fabric wall, a similar expression of irritation on her
face. Disapproving bookends.

"All right, all right," the girl presses. She has a sort of
drunken insistence, as though they've all been swilling
beers rather than mugs of coarse lentil stew. "But, come on.
This isn't just any mountain, right? This is Mount-mother-
fucking-Everest. Tell me something that's not on any other
mountain."

"Yeti."

The word is spoken with perfect clarity, but it's so incongruous, so unexpected, that for a moment no one seems to understand.

"Yeti." The Sherpa who spoke repeats himself, then looks around at the other Sherpas. He has that wide-eyed questioning expression of someone who's interjected in a conversation and worried suddenly they've missed the actual topic. He looks to Maya, then says something in Nepali.

She answers, and they exchange a brief, heated conversation—or, at least, it sounds heated to Carrie's untrained ears. But whatever conversation is happening, it seems to pick up in intensity. Maya's voice has dropped to a low hiss, as if she's afraid of being overheard.

Carrie glances at Tom, questioning, searching for any indication of recognition on his face, because she knows he must understand at least a little of the language. But his expression is inscrutable, his eyes turned toward the tent's drooping ceiling, watching the rhythmic pulse of fabric in the wind. The tent's walls breathe, an in-and-out flutter. As if the lot of them have been caught in something alive and are just now realizing it; Jonah in the belly of the whale.

"Excuse me," the doctor says, looking uneasily around the assembled group. It seems now to have a stark contrast, divided neatly along a language barrier—the Sherpas and the white guys. "Did you say, yeti?"

The Sherpa—who, Carrie now realizes, is quite young, hardly more than a teenager, nods enthusiastically.

"As in, abominable snowman?" the doctor reiterates, and, for emphasis, holds up his arms, elbows cocked, hands twisted into claws as he pulls a grimacing face. "Raawr?"

Maya smirks. She shakes her head. "It's a story of our people," she says, gesturing vaguely at the assembled group. "Yeti. Metoh. The bear-man."

"Yeah, right. Big guy, white fur. Bigfoot's cold-weather cousin." The doctor lets out a hearty laugh, clearly thinking the Sherpas are having a go at him and inviting them to give it up and enjoy the joke now. But none of them are laughing, and he cuts the laughter off abruptly, uneasily. "You're not telling me you think he's real."

"Is real," the young Sherpa says, latching onto the word and nodding again.

"A Sherpa legend," Maya says slowly, choosing her words carefully. "Before white men came, we never climbed the mountain. Our people lived in her shadow, safe. The mountain is goddess, mother of world. Is Sagarmatha. Holy place. Metoh-kangmi is the mountain man, snow man. He belongs to the mountain. Understand?"

She glances around, takes the silence that follows as an affirmation, and continues.

"Metoh-kangmi—the yeti—is a guardian, serving the goddess. Protecting the mountain. We tell his story as a warning. We do not go where we are not meant, you see?"

Something gnaws at the back of Carrie's mind, something she knew, or thought she had known—some story about a Buddhist temple, a cursed expedition failing to heed the warnings. She remembers it in bits and snatches. Something she'd read in Sean's diary, maybe? Something he'd told her once? She has a sudden urge to pull his diary from her pocket, to read it over and search for the words.

"But people climb all over the mountain now," the Eagle Scout is saying. "I mean no disrespect. But, just. If the mountain's guard is supposed to be keeping us from climbing up here … where is he?"

"In old times," Maya says, looking suddenly very weary, older than her years. Her gaze falls contemplatively to the ground, where the mats and pads they've layered for flooring are lumpy and uneven over the stone and ice below. "Sagarmatha provided for us with rain, good crops. Protected us and watched over us. But the world has changed, now. The world is about money." She lifts a hand, rubs two fingers together. "Mother goddess, she gives us money now. We afford schools, hospitals, because outsiders come to climb the mountain."

Stated that way, unadorned and without artifice, the truth of the words pierces like a dagger.

"But it is not perfect. There is sacrifice. White men leave behind their trash, their … kyakpa, their shit. But Mother goddess is old and strong. You will not destroy her. When she is done letting people climb, then she will not allow them any longer."

"And in the meantime," Carrie says, not meaning to speak but finding the words spilling out all the same, "the mountain takes a sacrifice of its own, every now and then."

She thinks of Sean, lost somewhere on the mountainside.

She thinks of Ang, whom she had never met, whose face she cannot even imagine. His body disappeared from where it had fallen, swallowed by the mountain. The other dead, known by names or only reputation, who dot the snowy slopes and whose bodies sometimes go missing, or else are belched up far from where they'd initially fallen.

Maya looks up from the floor, meeting Carrie's eyes with a shrewd smile. "Yes. Sometimes it is so."

Altitude sickness and cerebral edema and hypothermia and snow blindness and all the rest, Carrie thinks; just words. Just explanations. Another attempt at colonization, rationalization, men making themselves feel better about forces outside their control. They give a name to it, and think that will contain it. Categorize it, thinking that will make it safe.

But she knows better. In that moment, meeting Maya's eyes, she understands what the others are still struggling to make sense of.

There is no such thing as an accident on the mountain.

There is only the goddess and her will, the sacrifices that fuel her. And she will always have the final say.

CHAPTER EIGHTEEN

Everest is not, in many ways, an especially challenging mountain to climb.

That is, ironically, grotesquely, the reason that so many have died on its slopes. It has a tendency to attract novices and people who have no business there. Making the summit is not a test of climbing skill but of endurance and—to an extent—good fortune. A lucky break in the weather, good climbing conditions, safety through the capricious land-scape of shifting ice and stone.

That's what Sean had said, in the weeks and months of training before he left for Nepal. He often chattered excit-edly about the trip, and Carrie had tried to listen, then taken away all the wrong messages from his enthusiasm. She took his insistence about the ease of climbing the mountain at face value, had chosen to see it as a bald truth. This would be an easy climb, she rationalized to herself. He would do it, and get it out of his system, and they could move on with their lives.

It was convenient to believe that. She didn't stop to think beyond it because she did not want to spend more time thinking about what he was actually doing.

Everest was full of first-timers and amateurs who had no business climbing a big mountain. Sean was a life-long professional. He would be fine. And more than that—he would be finished. He'd get it out of his system, realize how silly his obsession had been, and he could at last finally be done.

These were things she told herself while he was away. The comforts she clung to in an empty bed when he stopped calling from satellite phones to check in about his progress.

It's easy. He'll do it, and be done, and you can get on with your life.

And then, sometimes, in the darkness, the quiet doubt.

But what if he doesn't?

And the nasty reply, from some dark place deep down.

Then you won't have to worry about it anymore.

Now here she is, a first-timer, an amateur with no business being here. If he had died on the summit of K2 or Annapurna, she could not have followed. She would have been forced by inexperience to stay home, unable to scale the steep rock faces, unable to navigate the ropes or find the support of willing Sherpas. What would she have done, she wonders? Would she have been forced to accept what happened? Would she have stayed on the other side of the world and allow his body to lay where it had fallen? Could she have learned to be satisfied with that, if she'd had no other choice?

She cannot say. It's impossible to guess for sure. But it no longer matters.

Because the truth is, Everest is not an easy mountain. It is a deadly mountain, and if it lures climbers into a false sense of security at times, it punishes them at others for their hubris.

"This bit is tricky," Tom says, not for the first time, checking over the ropes. Despite the thick layers of clothing he wears as defense against the biting wind, Carrie can see the lines of tension crossing his wiry back, in the angle of his head, the way the tendons knot and bulge in his neck.

At the head of the team, Maya is testing ropes laid out by other Sherpas, tugging at ice screws fixed into the steep wall they will momentarily be ascending. Pemba and Lopsang follow, heads lowered against the weight of their packs, laden with tents and camp stoves and bottles of oxygen.

"Tricky," Carrie echoes, and almost laughs.

"You know what I mean." Tom sighs, backing away from the ropes. "It's not quite a vertical wall. There's still definitely a slope. Keep an eye on where your crampons are going, lean on your legs rather than the ropes, take it one step at a time, and you'll be okay. I'll be right behind you the whole way."

For once, she finds that she's not bothered by his mother-hennish obsessing, nor the worried look that has settled in his deeply weary eyes. He looks small, vulnerable. She nearly reaches out to touch him, wanting to extend some small reassurance. But she does not. Instead, she turns toward the path and begins to climb.

There'd been a time, fleeting now in hindsight, when Carrie had believed she could become a mountaineer like Sean. It had not been her natural ambition. She never caught herself staring wistfully at mountains, imagining herself climbing them, never felt a thrill of desire at the risk and reward of climbing. But it was a thing that Sean loved, and by learning to love it as well, she'd hoped to get closer to him. Climbing was such a vital part of his life. It took up so many months of his years. It drove his career and his hobbies and shaped his body and she was certain that there was no real way to know him without understanding it.

So she convinced herself that she could learn to love it the way he did.

He was certainly an enthusiastic teacher. She'd been worried about that at first, that he would grow impatient with her or else that he might become defensive of his beloved hobby and try to hoard it for himself. Men were like that sometimes, Carrie knew—prickly and over-cautious about what they shared, unwilling to let anyone in past the walls built up around the things they held dear. But Sean was never like that. He was never anything less than enthusiastic about stoking the flames of her would-be interest, and in its way, that made everything a thousand times worse.

If not for the gentle encouragement, the enthusiastic support as she tried on climbing gear or attempted the next difficulty level at the indoor climbing wall or booked a weekend hike, she might have given up early. She might have found some other way to define their relationship, to fit her life against his, to find the edges of their separate puzzle pieces and lock into place. But his excitement at her interest melted her, and she poured herself around his edges like she could reform her life to mold around his. And by the time she realized she was miserable, it was too late to change. The dynamic was locked in place, their roles cast in the drama of their lives, identities solidified.

They honeymooned in Japan at the end of July, peak climbing season for Mt. Fuji.

She knew, of course, that they would be going in summer, but her mental image was still a composite of anachronistic photographs and impressions. She imagined tree-lined streets bursting with pastel pink and white, cherry blossoms falling gently in a delicate wind. She imagined busy streets filled with men in business suits and teenagers in school uniforms, eager-eyed tourists jostling for photographs with costumed mascots outside of landmarks. Shopping. Food at a high-end restaurant or a street vendor or a hole-in-the-wall ramen shop with sticky counters and broth so thick and savory she could almost taste it through her imagination.

When the plane touched down in Tokyo, Carrie and Sean stumbled out onto the tarmac, blinking and disoriented. Her head ached terribly. She'd barely slept on the flight, kept awake by Sean's restless fidgeting to one side and the sounds and smells of a child being sick across the aisle. Jet lag felt like a hangover, and she barely remembered the ride to the hotel, or even how the hotel had looked; she was face-first in the bed and mostly comatose for the next twelve hours, an inauspicious beginning to what she'd imagined as the first week of a new life.

Tokyo was dirty the way every city is dirty. Chicago should have prepared her for it, but you never notice the way your home smells, or see the trash and grime collected in gutters or blowing across the street. She was accustomed to the city's inherent grunge, could see past it to the unique and beautiful details. But every flaw in Tokyo felt magnified and exacerbated. The first time out of the hotel, attempting to make their way to Shibuya, they'd gotten turned around and boarded the wrong train by accident. They ended up in Shinjuku station, surrounded by milling crowds, packed in so densely that moving through them was like fighting a current. While Sean tried to figure out where they'd gotten turned around and how to get back, Carrie was separated from him, buffeted by the crowd, pushed to a grubby corner of the train station.

Surrounded by strangers, the white noise of voices around her in words she didn't understand, she felt agonizingly isolated. What if she didn't find her way back to Sean? What if she didn't find the hotel? Three young men in school uniforms passed her. One, his hair bleached orange, suit jacket draped over his shoulder, turned his head as he passed, his eyes roving down Carrie's body, and her heart leaped into her throat. He hesitated, like he was thinking of stopping, like he was thinking of something to say, but she slid sideways through a passing group of tourists and found Sean and it should have been fine from there.

But it wasn't, somehow. Her nerves never stopped jangling.

For the rest of the journey, wherever she looked, she could see only garbage and grime. Her gaze strayed naturally to the stray sheets of newspaper trampled by shoeprints, or cigarette butts collected in gutters, or glimpses of tattoo ink under shirt cuffs, or red-faced foreigners making a scene. Like a colored lens overlaying her perceptions, every aspect of her dream Japanese vacation was filtered through a negative light. And as the days counted down to their journey up the slope of Mt. Fuji, it only worsened.

She was in no mood for a hike. She was tired and crabby and wanted nothing more than to stay behind in the hotel room and sulk, spend a little time mourning the death of her high hopes and expectations. But she resisted the urge, not wanting to start a fight with Sean. Because, in her current mood, a fight would have been inevitable. And that would have only made their overall situation even more unbearable. He was still in good spirits, incorrigible in his enthusiasm, and she wanted so badly to find it charming and infectious but instead could not help but see it as tedious.

They walked down to the bus stop and climbed on, packs in their laps, watching the scenery outside whip by on the two-hour drive to Kawaguchiko 5th Station, from which they'd start climbing. The scenery twisted and blurred at the edge of Carrie's awareness, her patience for sightseeing eroded. She let herself doze and dipped in and out of muddled dreams, heavy on sensation, about winding stony trails. By the time they arrived at the station, she felt like she'd climbed Mt. Fuji a dozen times over. Facing its reality felt impossibly daunting.

But they climbed. As part of a crowd at first, a tour group clustered together at the start who slowly spread and scattered as they began their way up the slope.

"No need for ropes up here," Sean told her, by way of making conversation. He'd either failed to notice her waning enthusiasm or was compelled not to care; nothing seemed to make him flinch from his good mood. "No fancy footwork. A perfect beginner mountain. And the view! We'll stop off for the night at one of the mountain huts. It's like a way station. Plenty of futons on the floor for sleeping. Then we'll wake up early and make that last little push in time to catch sunrise from the summit."

"Sounds wonderful," Carrie said through gritted teeth, keeping her gaze fixed on the path directly in front of her, blood rushing like the ocean in her ears. She'd forgotten, or maybe had never known to begin with, that they would be staying the night. That two days would be eaten by this

12,380-foot volcano, uninvited third wheel to their honey-moon. They'd make the journey in seven hours today. Five to descend the next day. A day to recover from the effort. And then it would be back on the plane, back to real life, honeymoon is over, time for the real work to begin.

Now, widowed and half-frozen on the murderous slopes of Mt. Everest, Carrie wishes she could look back on this moment with pride.

She wishes more than anything that she could have mustered enthusiasm. Lost herself in Sean's excitement. Learned to love things, then, the way that he loved them, with his whole heart, instead of her usual brittle way that could be so easily shattered by minor disappointments. She wishes that she could say she climbed Mt. Fuji with him, hand-in-hand, and watched the sun rise over Japan, the sky painted crimson and indigo and reflected with perfect sym-metry in the lake below. She wants so badly for that to be her memory, good times shared with the man she loved.

But what she actually remembers is her willpower break-ing.

What actually happened was the last of her patience snapping, two hours into the hike, the summit impossibly, agonizingly out of reach and already a stabbing pain in the muscle of her leg. Already a miserable shakiness in her joints and a hollow twisting in her belly, the knowledge that she did not want to be here and did not want to do this coiling and twisting like snakes around the dawning realization that she was unfit for it even if she'd wanted to. An hour later she stopped, bent over and panting, and tried to will herself to keep going, only to find that all of the willpower left within her was circling the drain. She didn't want this. She had never wanted it, had only agreed to it under some mistaken idea that it would be easy, or at least tolerable.

"I can't do this," she said.

"Take five," Sean reassured, but there was an edge of impatience in his voice, the first hint of his good cheer finally reaching the end of the line. "Drink some water. Talk to me. What's going on?"

"I just can't," she repeated, and in that moment, she wasn't entirely sure what she was referring to.

The mountain? Japan? This marriage? They all seemed jumbled up together into one thing, now, and all of it was miserable. And what she wanted, more than anything, was for Sean to see that misery and relent. For him to agree to give it up and the two of them to go down together and salvage what was left of the trip before they had to go home and find a way to settle into married life.

"It's as far to the mountain hut as it is the road back to the hotel," Sean said. "You might as well finish it. We'll take it slow."

His math was broken, or else he was brazenly lying to her face, and she gritted her teeth together and stared at some weeds sprouting up between packed dirt and small stones on the path. She said, "I want to go back. I hate this." And then, primed by the inertia of her frustration, the rest came out in an avalanche. "I've hated everything about this trip since we got here. I'm fucking miserable and I never wanted to climb this stupid mountain and I don't even *like* climbing, I don't know why you keep forcing me to fucking do this."

Her throat, thankfully, closed up with a mounting frustrated sob, choking off any further protestation before more words could escape. Before she could say anything else she didn't mean or, worse, admit that maybe she'd meant all of them.

He was silent a moment. He crouched beside her, eye level, even as she stubbornly kept her gaze averted. She peeked sidelong through knitted lashes, blinked away the blur of moisture. Sniffed.

"Okay." He reached for her hand, his long knobby fingers closing over hers. He tilted his head up, casting a last look at the path they would be abandoning, the peak everpresent but invisible at scale. He thought for a while, like he was doing some mental calculation, like he was preparing to finish a project. She saw his tongue run over his chapped lips, saw the twitch of his beard along his freckled cheeks as his expression shifted and settled on a sad smile. "I didn't realize. I'm sorry."

She withdrew her hand from his grasp, swiped at her damp cheeks. She tried to pull away from him, but he shifted his weight, settling onto his haunches next to her, sliding an arm around her torso. He laid his head on her shoulder.

She waited for him to ask if she was sure. She waited for him to give her a chance to try to take it back. He said nothing, and she didn't either, and after a long silent pause he stood up and extended a hand to tug her back to her feet and when he started moving it was back the direction they had come.

It was dark by the time they made it back to the hotel, and she was tired and sweaty and had an awful headache from dehydration between the climb and the crying. She took two painkillers and stayed under the hotel shower stream as long as she could stand it, half-hoping maybe Sean would come in to keep her company, that maybe they could talk, but he didn't. When she came to bed, she slid in next to him in the sheets and laid her head on his bare chest. His fingertips brushed the damp skin of her upper arm as she fitted herself against the hollow between his arm and body. It felt okay, then. Safe. All she'd wanted, really. Just that reassurance, just that quiet moment's chance to catch her breath and reorient herself, and maybe this trip could be salvaged after all.

"Let's go tomorrow," she mumbled into his skin. "Let's change the tickets and stay another week and get a do-over."

"You have work."

"Fuck work."

"You don't have to pretend for me." He kissed the top of her head. "It's okay. Let's talk in the morning."

They slept, and talked about nothing of consequence in the morning. They shopped in Shibuya and got an over-loaded parfait, toppings spilling indulgently over the rim, and shared it. Sean would come back to Japan, years later, and bag Mt. Fuji with a group of climbing friends. He stopped asking Carrie to come along with him. No matter how often she tried to walk back her mountain slope confession—how many times she insisted she'd spoken in anger, that it was fine, that she could handle the climb, that she wanted to go, for real—it had stopped being a thing they did together. She'd still climb with him on the wall at the gym sometimes, would still run with him on trails sometimes when he was training. But something had broken irrevocably between them on Fuji.

The valley that cradles Camp II rises in a gentle slope before reaching a steep cliff, the Lhotse Wall. It's as if the mountain has remembered after a delay that it was meant to rise and has hastily over-compensated. The cliff is covered in ice, more glacier than stone, and it thrusts upward at an angle slightly steeper than forty-five degrees. Its surface is sliced through with cracks, some deceivingly narrow, others wide and gaping. Ladders have been set across these, the same as those in the Icefall—unsteady bridges clamped into the ice with metal teeth, slippery rungs offering the only defense against tumbling down into the waiting jaws of a mountain.

They climb in silence, because there is not enough oxygen to support both the effort of speech and of climbing.

At moments like this, when struggling against the forces of gravity, Carrie realizes why most of the climbers she's met have been so small. Unlike other athletes, size offers no advantage on the mountain. Hauling extra weight, even from muscle, makes an exhausting difference in this environment. She's grateful now of her own stature. She'd felt too thin when she arrived, delicate and spindly and far too easily broken. But the thinness poses an advantage now. She

cannot see the shift of muscle under the layers of her parka
and underclothes, but she feels them gliding over bone and
sinew, straining with effort.

Sean would have struggled with this all his life, she realizes, with a bittersweet recognition that she'd never once
considered this before. Sean was not a big man, but he had
been tall, with long limbs and broad hands. His build was
good for rock climbing—he could reach for difficult grips
and haul himself around like some agile spider—but it must
have been a struggle simply to heave that lumbering frame
against the downward forces of gravity.

She is thinking of this, imagining him crawling up this
slope, seeing the outline of his gangling frame and trying to
remember the exact shape of his silhouette, when her foot
slips on a ladder.

She lets out an inarticulate noise, body swaying backward as her foot slides forward, the crampon missing the
rung that is meant to hold it in place. She flails her arms
wide, pin-wheeling, and begins to over-balance, leaning
forward. The ground hurtles toward her, the yawning grave
of a crevasse growing ever larger in her field of vision.

She will fall. She will be pulled into the deeps like Ang,
swallowed by the gaps in the ice. She will snap her neck on
the descent, feel the crunch of bone and sinew and then feel
nothing, nothing at all—

No. She knows what to do. Her body knows.

The ladder beneath her shifts, tilting sideways with her uneven weight. She feels the tension in the rope clipping her into the line, and she leans against this tension, pulling it taut to counterbalance as she thrusts out the ax in her right arm, hooking it into the ice. She balances her weight that way, her body forming the third part of a triangle made by the safety line and the ax, and she uses these two elements to regain her balance and, a moment later, her footing.

Her crampons fit neatly between the rungs of the ladder-bridge. She takes a step forward, still leaning hard into the rope, the ax, regaining her center of balance. She bends low against gravity and leaps clear of the trembling ladder, thrusting the clawed toes of her boots into the crust of ice, finding a small ridge where she can stand without fear of falling.

The tension in the rope eases, slightly. Maya, anchored by an ax as well overhead, turns to look down at her.

Carrie cannot see the woman's eyes, or even read her expression. She is only peripherally aware of anyone near her. Her body sings with adrenaline, her muscles trembling with effort, and she shakes as she dislodges the ax and fights against her impulse to collapse panting into the snow.

It is not safe to stop here.

She cannot afford to linger.

Behind her, the crevasse seems to grow narrower, as if the waiting mouth were starting to close in disappointment that it would have no fresh prey to swallow.

"Carrie?" Tom, of course, at her side, having navigated the tricky ladder in moments. Balanced precariously next to her on a ledge barely big enough for one. His voice sounds strangled and distant behind the mask and regulator delivering the supplemental oxygen.

A touch, as if from far away. She is only peripherally aware of her body. It's a place she dwells in, sometimes, but not a place she owns. At the moment, all she knows is the flood of effort, the thrill of survival hormones, a chemical giddiness surging through her. She fights the urge to laugh.

She cannot explain it to him, but maybe she doesn't need to. Maybe he already knows.

The threat of death is nothing compared to this feeling. This fleeting, momentary feeling where nothing outside of her matters. The absolute peace of living in a world defined entirely by her body and the forces that stand in its opposition.

Her mind has gone blank and fuzzy, and it is exquisite.

Her body moves as it is trained, as she has done these many long weeks on the mountain. She finds safe footholds. Her grip is strong despite the numbness in her fingers. Her body moves where she tells it to go, and she feels so minimally invested in it, so distant, so calm. Her mind is a control room now, dictating her body's movements at a distance, and she guides herself to safety on the far side of the crevasse.

It will occur to her later, as she struggles to finish the last few agonizing steps of the climb up the Lhotse Wall, that in this moment she was not thinking of Sean or Chicago or what had broken between them in Japan. That she was not thinking of anything at all.

And in that realization, that brief glimpse at the exhilarating silence of a mind forced into absolute focus against the threat of death, she will finally begin to understand what it is that drives men to conquer mountains.

CHAPTER NINETEEN

Sean's travel diary, dated May 18

Several pages before this entry have been torn out

We've reached it—that tipping point beyond which it no longer makes sense to turn back.

Maybe that's nonsense. Tom would berate me for that kind of thinking if he were here. He's always been the sensible one. He'd tell me, "Sean, it's never too late to turn back. If you're ten feet from the summit and you can't keep pushing, you stop. You turn around. You do what you need to get home safe."

He'd say that, but we both know it's bullshit. If you're minutes away from collapsing ten feet from the summit, you're not getting home safe anyway.

Coming down is just as hard as climbing. Harder, actually. Most climbers who die do it on the way down. Because by then, you've done it. You've gotten the achievement. You've spent every last ounce of yourself pushing for that moment and you just have to hope you can make your way home on whatever fumes are left in the tank. That you can trust your body to remember how to keep going after the desire has been satisfied, after the fire has gone out.

Marriage is like that, too, I guess.

Anyway, we're more than ten feet from the summit, and turning back would probably be the wisest thing. But I can't imagine doing it. I can imagine, dimly, the summit. Know the steps and the strategy between here and there, can count off the feet and measure the supplies and ration the oxygen. I know what the next few days will look like.

But I'm struggling to imagine anything on the far side of it. When I try to think of what the world beyond this mountain looks like, feels like, tastes like, all I can imagine is a vague and snowy darkness, a speckled gray like television static. It's silly to think this way. It's irrational. But I'm starting to feel like nothing outside of this mountain exists. I'm starting to question whether anything beyond this present moment has ever been real.

I'm letting my imagination get the better of me. It's stupid to be thinking like this.

There is nothing circling the tents in the darkness.

The world will still be there when I return.

I will finish this climb and come down and go home.

CHAPTER TWENTY

Camp III is filled with detritus left behind by previous expeditions, a graveyard of items abandoned and forgotten by those eager to make the summit.

Empty tents, wind-tattered and forgotten.

Bottles of oxygen, some empty, others partially filled.

Masks and climbing axes and broken gear. Personal effects discarded by climbers who could no longer justify the added weight of hauling them up the mountain.

Nestled on a narrow band of cliff, a shoulder of icy stone cradled between Everest's summit and its neighboring peak, Lhotse, the camp consists of tents precariously erected wherever they will fit, empty oxygen tanks poking up like tombstones from the ice between them. The wind is ferocious, biting and wailing. Tom warns her that they'll need to lash themselves into place with ice screws and ropes while they sleep to keep from being blown down the face of the mountain when gusts crest over the ridge.

Carrie picks her way slowly through the camp, winded by the perpetual exhaustion of a body struggling against the thin atmosphere, but unable to quell her curiosity. She wants at least a cursory look through the things abandoned here. Wants to search, perhaps, for a clue of Sean's last night on the mountain, to find some hidden piece of him left behind among the garbage. Or wants simply to remind herself that this is the final stop, the last hold-out before the summit.

A cairn of stones stands not far from where Pemba and Lopsang have pitched the tents. The structure draws her eye. She's seen other monuments, less hastily erected, on the path here, but this does not look like those shrines. It looks like something made by inexpert hands, precariously balanced and barely standing against the wind.

The pile of fragmented rock stands waist-high, snow and dirty ice built up around it and seeping into the cracks between stones. At the base of the cairn, someone has left a photograph—its frame peeling, the glass cracked and clouded. Through the fogged-up glass, she can just barely make out the faded photograph of a woman smiling with something that might have been triumph, all big teeth and sun-chapped cheeks. In the photograph, the woman stands against a brilliant sky, the distant hints of peaks and clouds blurring together far behind her.

Maya comes behind her. Carrie feels the question in her eyes without even turning to look, she's grown so accustomed to the Sherpa woman's quiet stares.

"Who is this?"

"I do not know the name," Maya admits. She comes alongside, peers over her shoulder. Her gaze is trained on the stones, not the photo. "A climber who did not make it down."

Carrie backs away from the cairn. It has not occurred to her until this moment that the stones have been piled as something more than a monument—that somewhere beneath them could be the remains of a body, stripped by cold and dry air but preserved, mummified by the mountain. Knowing that she is standing within feet of a dead woman sends intermittent thrills of repulsion and fascination, the attraction of magnetic fields that yearn but cannot connect.

"But how can that be?" she finds herself asking, voice rasping from a throat torn raw by cold, dry air. "This is ... the camp is right here."

Maya shrugs. "Mountain is dangerous. You know."

She does know. And though she had asked, Carrie's mind is quick to think of many explanations for this woman's unfortunate demise. Perhaps she died of edema, some kind of swelling that took hold too quickly for her to be taken down to safety—like the fallen climber. No helicopter could land safely here. She would have had to be hauled down by hand, and what if no one were up to the task? Or perhaps she had been injured. Caught in a storm, dying of exposure here so close to shelter and warmth. Maybe she fell in the night, just feet from where other climbers would have lain sleeping and unaware of her struggle.

"This photograph," Carrie asks, hesitantly. "This is a summit picture, isn't it?"

Maya nods.

"From the same expedition, do you think? That she died on, I mean."

"Could be. Could be from another time—I could not say."

There's no way of knowing, of course, but Carrie has the strange and creeping feeling that it was from the same journey. That this nameless woman, known only by her smiling face, had summited the peak only to die on the way down, memorialized now, eternally, with her final great achievement.

That someone had developed the photograph, framed it, and carried it with them up this same mountain to lay it beside her. That someone had come all this way to mark her passing, because she would never leave the mountain.

Is this the way she would have wanted to be remembered, Carrie wonders?

Did she come here with the knowledge that she would not return? Was there someone left behind, spouse or children or dear friends, who had heard her wishes and been at peace with them?

Carrie would love very much to speak with them, these phantom loved ones conjured by her imagination. She wants to know how they did it. Where had they found their peace? What was it that finally allowed them to let go?

CHAPTER TWENTY-ONE

The journal is small, and Carrie has no intention of leaving it behind. It will not join the detritus, the abandoned gear and garbage and memories that litter the ground of Camp III.

All the same, it troubles her to carry it. Where once it had felt comforting to imagine its pulse, now she holds it close to her chest and feels only the unnerving certainty that it is breathing. That its leather covers rise and fall subtly against her hands or chest.

It's the missing pages that frighten her most.

The missing pages—and the way that final page looks, the sharp contrast with the others. Sean, always so careful, so tidy and meticulous with his notes. And then ... that. That single page with its manic, disjointed scrawl.

What was that about?

What was in those missing pages that could explain the change?

But if she's being honest with herself, the last page is not the only troubling part of the narrative. The pages are shot through with frightening signs from beginning to end. The description of Ang's death, that prowling figure outside the tent. The event with Maya—or whoever or whatever he had actually encountered, or thought he had encountered.

Carrie had consumed the diary happily enough at first, uncritically pleased just to have Sean near her again in some way. To soak them up as the last and most vital part of his identity. But now that it's over, the empty pages at the end ominously unfilled, she cannot continue to ignore their contents. Not when she is facing the possibility of finding him, or of never finding him. Not when she is so close to the goal of letting him go—and that's why she's come here, isn't it?

"You should get some sleep."

Tom's voice fills the darkness of their shared tent. Carrie is uncomfortably aware of his proximity, their shoulders bumping against one another through the sleeping bags. Two mummies wrapped for shipping and strapped down against the howling wind. She rolls over, grimacing at the jab of sharp stones felt through the tent floor and padded bed roll. She squints into the dark, trying to make out his face, seeing only the outlines of shapes. Tom has ice in his beard, the fog of his breath settling and freezing in the fine hairs at his chin, but warmth radiates off the parts of him not completely enshrined in layers of sleeping bag.

The wind cries beyond the tent walls. Carrie half-expects to make out voices in it, expecting—almost hoping—to hear the low growl of some creature lurking outside. It's better, somehow, to think that this monster might be real than to face that other option, the probability of Sean's madness.

"Sorry," she says, because she realizes Tom is waiting on her to respond. "I'm just. Thinking about Sean." A momentary beat, a pause as she contemplates whether to try and put words to the uncertainty that she feels. "Something he wrote in his diary."

She cannot read Tom's expression in the dark, but she can feel it. The air between them goes cold, somehow, in a way that has nothing to do with the howling winds outside.

"I'm sorry you had to read that."

He speaks with familiarity, as if knowing exactly what she's talking about. That realization makes her sit up. Pain shoots through her elbow, jabbed into the stony ground, but she ignores it. Ropes dig at her belly, the security lashings sliding painfully down her body as she rapidly changes position, but she ignores those too. She seeks out his silhouette in the darkness. Tries to pin her gaze on his eyes. "What?"

Tom hesitates, caught out now. Exposed. "The climb … the altitude. It can … do some things to your brain. Make you see things that aren't there. I'm sorry that you had to see him that way. That's not … it's not what I would have chosen for you."

"Did you read it?"

"What?"

"The diary. You're talking like you read his fucking diary."

Silence between them. The rustle of a sleeping bag as Tom struggles to evade her cold stare despite the darkness. As if he can feel her eyes even if he cannot see them.

"You never told me that you read it. How is that even possible? How did you get your hands on it?"

"It was … " he hesitates again. She can almost hear the ticking of his thoughts, like a machine trying to calculate a difficult equation. "Yes. I knew about the diary. Maya gave it to me. I read it, and I gave it back to her, and I told her to burn it."

"Are you fucking serious?"

Despite the wind ripping at the tent, despite the safety line lashing her down into her sleeping bag, Carrie is tempted to rise and leave. To walk out into the frozen darkness and find somewhere else to be. She would have tried her luck with a yeti rather than listen to him speak another word. But her body resists the demand. Self-preservation holds her in place, her limbs unwilling to coordinate with her desires.

"I didn't know what it was, at first," Tom replies, almost sulking. "Maya showed it to me. We were going over supplies for the expedition, before you got here, and she told me she had some of Sean's things. She didn't know what it said, so she asked me about it."

"And you just decided that I didn't need to read it. You decided what was best for me. Like you always have."

"That's not true." His voice goes low and cold, wounded. "If I did, you … you wouldn't be here."

"You always asked why I chose Sean," Carrie snaps, trying to roll over to face away from him. The hard, stony ground beneath the tent jabs into her shoulder as she heaves her body sideways. There will be bruises by morning, but she hardly notices the pain through the cold and anger. "This is it. Sean could be a dick sometimes, but he never thought he knew me better than I did."

"Sean didn't know you at all," Tom shoots back, heat rising in his voice, lifting the volume and intensity. It competes with the wind, a shout that threatens to carry well beyond the whipping of the tent. "He sure as shit didn't know what you were doing, did he? What *we* were doing?"

She shrugs down into her sleeping bag, desperate to escape this conversation, knowing there's nowhere for her to go. In the darkness, her gaze seeks out the zippered doorway of the tent. She tries to imagine some plan, some alternative to lying here and listening to this. A gust of wind, as if responding to her consideration, ripples against the nylon wall. The tent shivers and rises slightly from its spot, straining against the ice hooks staking it in place. Air rushes under and around the tent floor, each gust rocking her body upward like a car going too fast over a bump.

"I never told him," Tom continues. There is a rustling, the sound of his weight adjusting in the sleeping bag. "And I wanted to. You fucking know I wanted to."

"It wasn't worth it." She swallows hard, tries to force back the tears that threaten at the back of her eyes. Crying will take up too much precious oxygen. She cannot bear to have them freeze in streaks to her face, for frost to crust her lashes. Her body is too exhausted to deal with this. The adrenaline that would normally shoot through her at the first sign of conflict is woefully sluggish to respond, all used up by the daily struggle of survival. Instead she feels only a deep and empty ache that spreads through her body and settles in her bottomless gut. "It was one time. It wouldn't have lasted."

"One time." He snorts, making a disgusted sound at the back of his throat. "You're just as deluded as he was."

Tom had been safe.

Safe, reliable, boring Tom. The embodiment of what-ifs. The guy she could have met in that bar in Argentina—the one she should have met, the one who was looking for love to begin with. If he hadn't been in the bathroom when she walked past, if she'd met him instead of his red-haired wingman, what would have happened? What would her life have looked like now?

That was the question she always asked herself when things got bad with Sean. Those times when he withdrew into himself, refusing to talk, or else when he ran away to the mountains, disappearing for hours or days or weeks at a time, evading her questions and discussion and responsibility.

Would it have been different with Tom?

Would it have been better?

"I would have quit climbing for you." He seems to address her, but his tone suggests he's talking mostly to himself. "I was ready. Me and you. We could have made this work. We would have been happy. Shit, Sean would have been happy. Everyone could have had what they wanted."

It had been more than once.

It had been often enough that she came to know the shape of his body in the dark. Enough that she became familiar with the gentle probing question of his touches and his patience, a conscientiousness she was unused to and found unsettling.

He had been safe, and she had not wanted safety—not really.

"But we didn't." Carrie's voice comes out muffled by the thickness of her sleeping bag. "None of us got what we fucking wanted, did we?"

Sean is gone, and Carrie needs Tom with her: needs him to absolve her guilt. To take her to the top of the world where she can escape the awful knowledge that she somehow caused this. Tom was complicit, and he needs to atone as much as she does—but here he is, acting like what they shared was real. Acting like he didn't know how things would have ended for them.

"No." Tom hesitates. A catch of breath, as if he's about to say something and cuts himself off with a sharp intake of air instead. He falls silent, panting against the thin atmosphere, and though it's hard to hear under the insistent whipping of the wind, Carrie is sure she can detect some irregularity in his breathing. The hitch of a quiet sob.

"We should sleep," she says quickly, setting her jaw against the finality of the words. She does not have the energy to fight, not here, not now. With the depth of the exhaustion in her body, she isn't sure that she'll ever have the energy to fight again.

THE BOURNE

CHAPTER TWENTY-TWO

As they huddle at Camp III, fighting the bitter winds and preparing to carry their search higher into the mountain— into that no-man's land where they will only have a two or three day window to look for Sean before being forced to retreat—another expedition has begun its descent. The climbers stop to camp on the stony shoulder between Everest and Lhotse, huddled against the wind alongside Carrie's group.

There is little time or space for socializing at this elevation, but Carrie catches a glimpse of one climber outside his tent, pawing through his pack with an expression of alarm as if he has lost something. He is short and thin, his body practically emaciated by the effort of his climb. He wears a blue down jacket and knit cap pulled tight around his ears, curls of dark hair spilling out from beneath.

"Everything okay?"

He looks up, startled. There is something glazed and un-steady about his gaze, as if he is not entirely sure that he's looking at someone real. "Yeah. I'm just." He gestures vaguely at his pack, then shifts sideways, sitting down hard on the snowy ground near the mouth of the tent. The way he moves his body suggests deep exhaustion, as if every move-ment is occurring at the barest edge of his strength.

If he were left here alone, Carrie wonders, would he be able to get back?

Or would he sit down like this and surrender to the cold and exhaustion?

"Are you coming down from the summit?" she asks, re-alizing that she's more curious than she'd expected to be. Realizing that, while she has little interest in the summit herself, she craves stories from those who have touched the roof of the world—who have been where Sean was, accom-plished what he had, who had heeded that insistent whisper that still rises in the back of her mind from time to time.

Summit. Summit. Summit.

He grins, but it's an empty smile, going through the mo-tions as he pulls his lips back from his teeth. "Nobody ever talks about coming back down."

She nods. That seems right.

"You reach the top and it's supposed to be this big achievement. You're supposed to be changed by it. But you can only stay up there for a few minutes. You're so fucking tired you don't even care where you are. And then it's the way down, and there's no glory in getting off a mountain."

In the weeks following Sean's disappearance, there had been a flurry of news articles posted about the story, listing him among the dead for the season—his name alongside an eighty-six-year-old record-seeker who had a heart attack at Base Camp, a pair of climbers from India who fell to their deaths when their ropes came loose, a woman who collapsed with cerebral edema. As if they had all been the same. As if every death on the mountain could be so neatly summarized and categorized.

One of the things the articles shared in their reporting was a statistic that the majority of climbing deaths occur on the way down, not the push for the summit. Exhaustion and carelessness are the main reasons frequently cited.

But Carrie has been here long enough to think that, maybe it isn't about being tired.

"It's like something doesn't want me to leave," the man says, startling her—as if reading her mind.

She creeps closer, rapt and afraid. "My husband died on this mountain," she says, dropping her voice as if they were co-conspirators. "He reached the summit last year but never came down."

"Is that so?" The man in the beanie tilts his head. His eyes are heavily shaded beneath his brows, the dark brown of his irises fading into the black of his pupils to create an unnerving depth to his gaze, like two bottomless pools in the dark. "You know what he was wearing?"

That is not the question she expects him to ask, and it catches her off guard. She struggles to remember. When someone is lost, that's the first thing to recall—but it's not like she had been making posters, stapling them to poles in Nepal. "Red, I think," she says, finally. He bought new gear for the trip. They'd fought over the expense. She remembered that much. But what had it been? Had she ever seen him in it?

He had promised her a selfie from the summit, but it had never come. Erratic signal, she guessed.

"I think he was wearing red," she asserts.

The climber nods, looking thoughtfully at one gloved hand as if he is not wholly convinced that it belongs to him. "I saw somebody wearing red up there. Just under the Hillary Step. Hard to see on your way up, with how the angles work—but on the way down, they're right there. Red coat and, I think, red hair? Pretty sure. It's hard to tell at a distance. But I saw them off the path, half-buried in the snow. Looks like they took a tumble off the step and got hung up in ropes, maybe. Or maybe I was seeing things wrong."

Carrie feels something in her chest shudder and seize, as if her heart is being squeezed painfully. A war between hope and terror rising to fill her body.

She gets him to repeat everything, to tell her again exactly what he'd seen, where he'd seen it. To commit the description to memory. To sear it into her imagination.

Later, when she eagerly tells this to the others—disregarding even the uneasiness of Tom's proximity, the words they needed to share but haven't—Maya looks vaguely impressed. Tom's expression is skeptical.

"We'll look," he says, to still her protest. "But just … don't get your hopes up. We don't know anything yet." A hesitation, brow knitting. "Who did you say it was who told you?"

"I didn't get his name," she mutters. "White guy. Blue coat and hat. Dark hair."

Tom's eyes go wide. He exchanges a confused look with Maya.

"What?" Carrie demands, shifting uneasily.

"It's just. I don't think … " Again, Tom looks to Maya. She evades his gaze. "There was a call over the radio last night. Someone matching that description died near the summit. It's … just a weird coincidence, I guess."

Carrie's stomach coils into a knot, remembering the man's words. His confusion. The distant look in his eyes, like he wasn't even sure she was real.

It's like something here doesn't want me to leave.

In the Death Zone, there is no acclimatization.

Life simply is not meant to exist at the cruising altitude of an airliner. Above 26,000 feet, the air is too thin. The cold is achingly sharp, biting through flesh and down into the bone. Oxygen is thin and spread, molecules spaced too wide for lungs to capture them all. A visit to the summit of Everest is no less alien or inhospitable than a trip to the moon or the depths of the ocean.

These are the warnings Carrie has been given, the messages she has internalized, yet it still catches her by surprise when they reach Camp IV. She is not prepared for the subtle betrayals of her body: the deep exhaustion, the fuzzy-headed sensation of time delay and mental disconnect. It feels like being very drunk, the way it feels when the good times have ended but the alcohol still has control of your body. That moment when everything feels out of your hands and you wish you could just stop now, just stop being drunk, you've had enough of this please.

Funny, she realizes with a sense of detached bitterness, that she always used to end up in that situation when Tom was around.

But she is not drunk today and—fuzzy-headed or not—she is in control. That is what she tells herself, anyway, as she approaches Tom and Maya.

Summit, the voice at the back of her mind whispers. She tries to ignore it, or tries to pretend that she can ignore it.

"I want to go to the top."

" … What?"

"The summit. I want to climb to the summit."

Tom looks at her, dumbfounded. "You … want to climb to the summit," he echoes, in that way of his, the lilt of his voice that injects reason into his words, that twists them around to examine them with a sort of abashed skepticism. "After all this. All the time you insisted that you had no interest in it. You want to climb it now?"

Are you punishing me? He seems to ask with his eyes, but she does not avert her gaze.

Instead, she nods. She cannot find words to explain it, not against the scoffing rationalization in his voice. But she holds firm nonetheless.

Maya, at least, seems to understand. "She is wanting to see from the top of world."

"Sean was there," Carrie adds, almost ashamed to hear the way it comes out like a plea. "I … I may never get to see what happened to him. But I want to see what he saw, at least. And—" she adds, her voice rising, "if that guy was right, if there is a body under the Hillary Step, that you can only see from above. I want to see that, too. I want to look. But even if we don't find him, I want this trip to have been worth … something."

A curious expression crosses Tom's features, inscrutable but flickering almost like a smile—and then there it is, the smile itself, deepening the lines at the edge of his mouth and bringing light into his tired eyes. "All right," he agrees. "All right."

He sounds relieved.

Maybe this has been his hope all along. It occurs to Carrie in a distant way, a roundabout realization, that Tom had agreed to bring her here knowing she likely would never find Sean's body. Knowing that her purpose was futile, and that she would come eventually to realize it and give up the attempt.

There are few things Tom Fisher is truly good at in life, but one of the best is getting people to the top of mountains. Maybe he's known all along how this would end.

There is only a brief window for summiting Everest.

For a few days out of the year, the weather and the mountain reach a period of stasis and understanding. Before this point, it is too bitterly cold to attempt the ascent; climbing Everest in the winter is too impossibly deadly for people who already struggle against frostbite and hypothermia in the thin mountain air. After the climbing window closes, the mountain becomes inhospitable due to storms. Further down the slopes, among the valleys of the Himalayas, summer monsoons bring rain to water crops and bring life to forests. But summer atop Everest is nothing but howling wind and bitter lancing ice, snow threatening to crumble down in deadly avalanches, glaciers melting and sliding and rearranging themselves to reinvent the mountain each year.

As the climate warms, summer grows longer and the climb becomes more treacherous, the window of safe ascent narrowing further with each year.

In the spring, then, there are only a few opportunities to reach the summit. A meager few days of perfect conditions. Thus, by necessity, every expedition bottlenecks on its way to the top.

At least, this is the explanation Carrie has been given for the rise in foot traffic between Camp III and Camp IV—people going up, but also those coming back. This stretch of mountain is more crowded than any she's seen since leaving Base Camp. People lined up on the ropes, climbing single file in queues that move so slowly they seem to be standing still. Less like climbing a mountain and more like waiting in line at a theme park, Carrie thinks, seeing the crowds of bodies jumbled together.

She and Tom have not spoken of anything but climbing since that night. She likes it that way. It is not worth expending precious oxygen on conversation, not when it must be measured and budgeted and carried as added weight. She avoids his gaze and focuses on the tasks at hand: melting snow for tea, securing ice hooks for ropes, examining climbing gear for damage. Managing her life through the logistics of hunger and thirst and safety. These logistics fill hours that she might otherwise try to spend thinking or worrying.

Climbing creates its own worries, and pushes all else from the mind.

Camp IV marks the final border between the habitable mountain and the Death Zone. Even with oxygen, there is no camping in the Death Zone itself. The atmosphere is too thin. A body, exposed to such extreme altitude, will begin to succumb to self-destruction, cannibalizing its own tissues for sustenance after just a few hours. A day or two in the Death Zone would make the area hold true to its name.

And so, they will ascend the peak. They might linger at Camp IV, venture onto side paths, search for a body—a scrap of fabric, a glimpse of red hair—or they might retreat to Camp III to wait for the right window for the summit.

But sooner than she'd like, the summit window will close. The weather will warm, the muddy monsoon will soften the ice, the storming clouds will envelop the peak each afternoon. And when that happens, if they have not found Sean, they will be forced to turn around and go home. It will be over.

It has to be.

At Camp IV, Maya and Tom and Carrie crouch against boulders and pass around a map of the summit, discussing routes and plans. Pemba and Lopsang are elsewhere, too busy or distracted to care. But for her part, Maya seems interested—keenly so, Carrie thinks. Almost excited.

It occurs to her that, maybe, finding Sean means something to the Sherpa woman after all. Not the same as for her, perhaps, but something significant. Maybe in her way Maya is also looking for absolution for the sin of leaving a client on the mountain. Maybe she is looking for some kind of closure herself.

"We came from here," she's saying, prodding at the map with one fingertip. Her nail is dry and jagged, worn down and torn from repeated use at the end of a chapped and weather-worn finger. "Sean came down first, leaving from here. The route is here. Maybe he goes this way, or that." Tapping two places on the map.

Tom seems less invested. He nods and hums his agreement at all the right times, but his gaze keeps straying from the map, traveling upward into the thin blue sky, his mind perhaps straying to the summit and Carrie's newfound insistence upon it.

CHAPTER TWENTY-THREE

Sean's travel journal, final page; undated

Summit day.

SUMMIT DAY. SuMMiT DaY. SUMmit DAY.

Summit summit summit summit day.

Summit.

Day.

CHAPTER TWENTY-FOUR

No one will be making it to the summit this morning.

On Everest, a summit push must begin in the dead of night, teams climbing the final leg through the Death Zone in the dark. It's the only way to ensure that the weather will hold for the return trip. A late start means being caught out in the open, late-day sun softening the ice into a treacherous, slippery mess. Ice screws and ropes will not hold weight in the sweating glacier; crampons will not gain traction in the slush. And so, to make the ascent before the mountain re-shapes itself, climbers must rise shortly after midnight and begin their climb through the witching hour.

But not tonight.

It is obvious before midnight that the morning will not be safe. The weather on Everest is notoriously fickle, and though guides have methods of predicting it, attempting to impose reason and logic on an environment that refuses to be tamed, there are no assurances. For all the meteorological projections and estimations, storms sometimes come without warning, and that is the case tonight.

The winds come first, howling against the slope, tearing at the edges of tents. With them comes the cold, a sweeping drop in temperature that has its own presence, an oppressive weight that settles and spreads and seeks entry where it is unwelcome.

Lying in her sleeping bag, Carrie shivers in her sleep, that insidious cold cutting past the defenses of body heat and insulation to pierce her bones.

But it is not the cold that wakes her.

At Camp IV, climbers sleep with oxygen masks tight over their faces, the insistent hiss of air serving as a lullaby—white noise to drown out the howling wind. But in the darkness, Carrie awakens feeling suffocated, as though something heavy is sitting on her chest, wrapping one smothering hand over her face. In the darkness, she can almost see it—some shadowy presence, some catlike being covering her body, peering down at her with dark eyes set into a darker face.

She tries to take in a breath and finds that she cannot. She sucks uselessly for air, lungs screaming in protest. She is drowning on dry land. She is sinking into the depths of stony darkness, pulled under by invisible tides that seek to entomb her in the heart of the mountain.

She lifts a weak hand to grasp the mask covering her mouth and nose. Tugs it away, feeling the straps first yield, then give way entirely as she tears the apparatus from her face.

She breathes deeply, inhaling greedy mouthfuls of air, and her lungs sear with the cold. The relief is immediate, a rush of euphoria as the air reaches her brain. Like the first drag of a cigarette after a long withdrawal. Like taking off an immense weight and feeling weightless and sparkling and untethered by the newfound freedom.

She lies, panting, for what seems like a long time, merely relishing the simple pleasure of being able to breathe. But slowly, thoughts return to her.

The mask must be defective. Ice in the regulator, or some problem with the hose. A leak somewhere that had emptied the tank. Whatever the cause, the oxygen had failed. There had been no creature in the dark, no cat-shaped incubus made of darkness and breath-stealing malice.

There had to be more oxygen somewhere, didn't there? She tries to remember. She's certain she's seen the supply of extra bottles, but in her addled, sleepy mind, she struggles to remember where.

Tom sleeps fitfully beside her, making small and inarticulate noises muffled by the steady hiss of his own oxygen mask. He shifts, squirming in his sleep, but does not open his eyes. She does not want to wake him. Does not want his concern, and does not want his confirmation of what has been apparent all night: that in this weather, it will not be safe to climb by morning. Not to reach the summit, and not to look for Sean.

They will spend the day hunkered down in their tents, waiting for the storm to pass. If they're lucky, they might get a second shot tomorrow. If not, they will need to retreat to Camp III. And once they've done that, Carrie worries they will never again ascend. That Tom and Maya will conspire to come up with some sort of reason they cannot push ahead once more. The weather will not hold. They will run low on supplies. Somehow, for some reason, everything will be snatched away from her at this eleventh hour.

So she does not wake Tom.

Instead, she rises carefully from the mummy-style sleeping bag, extricating herself as quietly as she can. She sleeps fully clothed on the mountain, has grown accustomed to lying bundled in layers. She's nearly forgotten what her body looks like beneath it all. Has lost acquaintance with her flesh. If she comes down again, she thinks, if she ever returns to the world, she will need to shed these layers like a snake stepping from its skin, and then what will she be beneath?

Oxygen. She's losing track. Her head feels like a balloon, tossed about on the wind, threatening to rise from her shoulders and float away into the endless sky. Her thoughts jumble. She needs to find more oxygen.

In the Sherpa tent? Certainly. It must be there. Near the camp stove and the food stores. She will creep out into the night and look for it, and prove to herself that she can do even this one small thing to prove her ability to stay alive, to forestall the absurdity of suffocating, drowning to death at the top of the world.

She struggles with the tent zipper, pushing awkwardly through the flap, feeling like some kind of animal struggling and squirming to escape from a net. The tent grabs at her, catching at her clothes as if trying to hold her in place. It seems to take an eternity to shrug out of its grasp, and she stumbles, falls to her knees outside. She grimaces as a stone digs through the layers of her clothes and jams painfully into her leg.

But the pain brings clarity, and with clarity comes resolve.

The tent flap, caught by the wind, flutters insistently like a bird on a string. It snaps and strains, threatening to tear.

Tom, inside, makes a disgruntled noise, rolling over in his sleep.

Carrie hurries to her feet and struggles to get the flap closed again, sealing the tent off from the worst of the storm.

It has begun to snow. Flakes blow sideways, shards of ice that swirl and dance and slice. The whiteness blocks out most of the radiant sky, hiding its constellations and distant galaxies from view. There is only the ground ahead of her, whiteness swirling all around, and a dim ethereal glow from the moon reflecting through snow in the darkness.

It is beautiful and unearthly and terribly, awfully lonely.

In this moment, she cannot shake the feeling that she's the only person alive. That she has somehow been transported to some version of the world where she is all that exists. She and the mountain, locked in an uneasy embrace, the forces of her solitude bearing down from all directions.

She starts toward the Sherpa tent. She struggles to remember why she's out here. She's dizzy, disoriented in this empty and bitterly cold landscape, as desolate and alien as any other place man might seek and fail to conquer. The surface of the moon. A distant planet. The vast reaches of the Arctic. The depths of the sea.

There are fossils of shellfish embedded in the stone near the peak—she remembers that now. She'd read it once, maybe in a guide book in preparation for this trip. Maybe in one of the nature magazines Sean had written for. It didn't matter. But she remembers it now, keenly. The whole of this mountain had once been beneath the ocean, the earth forced upward to break free of the water's surface, mountains formed through the violence of colliding continents. The lowest points on earth rising tumultuously to become the roof of the world.

Why has she come out here, again?

Summit.

Summit.

Summit.

She freezes. The voice seems to come from within her, but also from the outside. It's as all-pervasive as the snow, as enigmatic as an echo in the darkness. She turns to look, and her body seems to move on a time delay. She has the strangest feeling that she's come disconnected from it, that her body is a marionette dangling from strings controlled by the hand of her consciousness, a puppeteer who moves with the deliberation of a god.

Summit.

Who is speaking?

Why is she here?

She stands dumbfounded in place beneath the swirling snow. Her jacket is partially unzipped, and snowflakes filter down into the open collar and catch against the fabric of her undershirt, not quite warm enough to melt through. She wears boots, but no crampons. She should probably put on crampons, she thinks. She should probably put on a hat. Her hair falls loose around her shoulders, a messy tangle, white-gold in the moonlight.

Summit, the voice whispers again, and this time she's certain that she sees it—a vague shape moving behind the snow, white-on-white in the swirling storm. Or perhaps it's the snow itself, gained sentience. Some vast whiteness, slow-moving but deliberate. It's hard to tell for certain what is mountain and what is snow and what is creature.

Perhaps they are all one and the same.

The thing moves, whatever it is. Carrie locks her gaze upon it and feels a growing sense of awe, nearly like reverence. It is giant, impossibly huge for something that manages also to be hidden. It's furry, too, or maybe that part is an illusion from the blowing snow. But it moves like a mountain would move, if a mountain could come alive.

It's not so very far away. It stands now just at the edge of camp, peering at her with eyes she cannot see but which she is certain can see her.

Summit, it whispers, and she realizes she wants very much to follow it. She has never wanted anything so much in her life.

She pulls away from the tents and, open-jacketed, boots half-laced and missing their crampons, pursues the thing in the darkness.

It leads her over an expanse of unmarked snow, pristine and glistening beneath the moon. However quickly she follows, it stays the same distance from her—a massive beast, its edges ill-formed through falling snow and thickening fog.

She follows this creature that moves like a mountain, and finds that her feet gain confidence with each step. She does not slip or struggle with the ice. Her muscles do not scream with the effort. Though the air is thin, the ache in her lungs seems to dissipate with each step—as though she is at last moving with the current, not against it. As though each step is bringing her in line with some common goal and all difficulty is peeling away.

They do not cross the paths already well-worn by the expeditions before them. Each footstep leads Carrie over the crust of untouched snow.

It's so easy, Carrie thinks, in a peripheral way that lingers at the back of her thoughts. It's so easy to walk here, easier than anything she has done since arriving in Nepal.

Why were these not the paths that they climbed? Did no one understand that this was the better way to travel the mountain?

She does not need the hooked crampons or fixed ropes or ice axe to maintain her footing. She needs only to follow the thing in the darkness.

She'd been out of breath when she awoke. She remembers that now, is vaguely aware of it, distantly confused by the sudden ease of her breathing. She does not spare it much thought. She breathes easily. She does not feel the cold.

The creature she follows is protecting her from it, somehow, shielding her from the bitter blast of the storm that tears along the ridge.

She tries to move faster so that she might catch up with her guide, but it keeps its steady pace at the edge of her vision, moving lightly over the surface of the snow in a way that leaves no tracks and makes no sound. Or perhaps it's the snow itself dampening the sound, muting everything until there is only silence and the insistent beating of her heart in her ears.

It's womblike, she thinks, as the creature leads her away from camp and upward in a gently sweeping arc toward the higher reaches of the mountain.

Like being an infant, warmly swaddled by the comforting damp, surrounded only by the sound of a heartbeat.

She has never felt so comforted in her life. She has never felt so at peace.

Carrie has the curious sensation of being able to see the path ahead of her, and also to see herself upon it, as if her awareness has risen up and to the right of her body. She looks down from a position somewhat overhead, watching her thin frame hidden beneath the thick down-filled blue parka, the tangles of her hair and the thin strands of silver working up from the roots.

She sees, too, another climber. Someone approaching from the side, though she does not know where they came from or how they came to be here. She is only aware of them from the part of her vision that has grown beyond her body, the part that belongs to the mountain itself.

She does not stop. She is afraid to stop moving, afraid that she will lose sight of the pale beast that leads her safely over the snow. She knows, somehow, if she loses track of it that she will be lost, that its protections will evaporate, that she will be agonizingly cold and alone.

And so she walks, inhabiting a place beyond pain or fear or exhaustion, following a giant that seems to grow neither near nor far but remains only at a fixed point ahead of her. The other climber reaches her side, falls in step with her. Her awareness floats behind them both in silence.

"Carrie."

A voice like the wind, a voice like a whisper in the dark. Like words whispered in a dream, and the disorientation of waking and wondering where they originated.

But it's a familiar voice, and she dares to pause, feeling her heart climb suddenly into her throat. Her consciousness, trailing behind her body, outstrips them both. For a moment, her vision flickers, affords her a birds-eye view. The world around her has gone dark, the fog and snow thickening to an oppressive blanket with only a spotlight shining its singular beam upon her.

There are only two things that exist here, in this moment, in this place.

"Sean."

He reaches out a hand, gloved fingertips tracing the lines of her face.

"You came for me."

"You can't be here."

"I have never been anywhere else." He smiles, that same self-conscious, sheepish grin that won her over so completely in Argentina, all teeth and bright eyes and freckles arranged into constellations over his lined cheeks. "It took a while for my body to find this place, but my soul has always been on this mountain. You know that."

She realizes that her feet have stopped moving. She has the feeling of being torn between movement and stasis, wanting desperately to follow the rapidly vanishing creature in the snow even as her body yearns toward Sean.

"I was following something," she feels herself say, stupidly. Her words slur as though drunk, speaking through heavy fog. "I'm going to lose it. We have to go."

Sean extends a hand, grasping for hers. His fingers curl around her gloved palm. Pressure, but not warmth. "It brought you to me," he says, and his voice is so reasonable that she cannot believe she had ever thought anything else. "Let it go, now. I have something to show you."

"Am I dreaming?" she asks, words heavy as they fall from her mouth. She stumbles forward, feet losing their coordination now that she is no longer walking in the protected path laid by the beast in the snow. "This isn't real."

In response, Sean pulls her close, covers her mouth with hers. Kisses her, his lips cold and firm like stone. Breath enters her lungs, fills her body. It tastes like him.

He lets her go and again takes her hand, tugging her forward. She follows. They walk for a time. Carrie is not certain who is leading and who is following, or if they both move somehow toward a predetermined location without knowing it. She does not know where they're going, but her feet once more feel certain upon the path. As long as she keeps hold of Sean's hand, she thinks, she will not stumble. She cannot fall.

She is distantly aware of the hammering in her chest, a feeling that might be fear or excitement or merely exertion as she walks hand-in-hand with this specter who cannot possibly be her husband, but is certainly no one else.

"I miss you," she says, finally, after what could have been minutes or hours. Although snow continues blowing around them, the wind has fallen silent, taking the sounds of the world with it until there is only her voice. She cannot hear the crunch of snow beneath their feet or the low, insistent moans of the settling weight of the mountain.

"I'm right here."

"You're not," she protests, and he responds with an insistent squeeze of his hand. She returns the pressure. She waits to awaken. It is not true after all what people always say—that you can feel nothing in a dream. Dreams can be painful. Dreams can be more real than anything. She knows this, and so waits to be woken, braces for the disappointment of being torn from him.

But he pulls her forward, and they walk over a crest of snow without interruption, his hand a solid, constant pressure in hers.

"It was snowing like this," Sean says, tugging her forward. "That night."

Carrie tries to remember whether she knew that before. She does not think she did. She would have known, probably, if it had been storming. Someone would have told her. But nothing seems certain now, as if past and present and future are all twined together to rewrite themselves.

"Tell me," she says.

And so he does.

CHAPTER TWENTY-FIVE

Sean

A part of me always wondered what it would be like to die of cold.

I think maybe that's something that every climber thinks about at some point. Of all the ways to die on a mountain, hypothermia sounds like the best. The least painful, anyway. They say the cold just makes you sleepy, and then you pass quietly into unconsciousness, drifting off into nothingness. They say it like it'll be painless.

They're fucking liars.

What no one tells you is the awful hours when your body is frozen but your mind is left awake, disconnected but painfully aware. You know about sleep paralysis? The way your body is held prisoner while you lie in bed, unable to talk or scream or move as dark things creep around in the night, standing in doorways or at the foot of your bed and leering down at you?

Freezing to death is a lot like that, except the things that watch you from the darkness are not from your imagination.

The storm came on us suddenly. It was not supposed to snow that day. No one could have seen it coming, not based on the weather the morning of the summit push. The sun rose that day in a bright, pale sky, cloudless and calm and terribly, bitterly cold.

I don't know what time the snow started. By then, I had already lost my way on the path. I spent a long time climbing down what I thought was the path back to camp, but I guess was curling around the peak in another direction, taking a spiral route down the western face. I climbed for a long, long while before I realized that I was not going down but rather around, working confusing circles around the face below the peak.

I don't know how I got so turned around. The elevation, I guess, messing with my head. But it began to feel like I was following someone, or something, and I remember feeling if I could get just a little bit closer that things would get easier. That I'd be able to catch my breath, finally.

I don't know when I fell. Or maybe I sat down, tried to take a break. I know that I couldn't get back to my feet. I sat there, feeling my body go numb, muscles growing stiff and inflexible, frost starting to form along my coat. I sat, and realized I could not stand, and the world grew more distant as my consciousness flickered but—I was aware.

I was aware up until the very end.

I heard and saw people moving past. They did not see me. I had nestled into an alcove, an underhang of rock and ice, and no one was paying attention. I could not call out; my mouth was frozen, my jaws locked in place. Only my eyes could move, tracking back and forth, tracing the shadows of people as they moved past my hiding place, the alcove that would become my grave.

I was alone. Snow began to fall, threatening to bury me here, and I have never been so isolated.

But I was not alone forever.

Or they had always been there, waiting silently and invisibly in the snow, biding their time until I was able to see them at last. They came and circled me and brought me to my feet, and I joined them, forever.

Because you see, Carrie.

You are never alone on this mountain.

CHAPTER TWENTY-SIX

Carrie realizes, as soon as Sean says it, that his words are true: they are not alone.

She does not know when the others appeared, but they surround them now, closing in on them in a loose circle. Here is a dark-skinned man, smiling wide, his teeth gleaming in a rictus grin. A woman, her skin pulled tight to her bones, hair falling loose around her shoulders. A short, slender figure whose fur-lined parka fully obscures its face, giving the impression of an empty coat that slumps forward toward them. A man dressed in old-fashioned tweed, his bloodless limbs white and knobby, a hole evident in the side of his head.

They stand clustered in the fog, a whole assemblage of them. A climber with brightly colored boots; a woman shambling up, still tangled in ropes. White men and women and foreigners and Sherpas, so many Sherpas, and they stream out of hidden corners and fill the spaces around them until the mountain itself is obscured. Their breath rises, creating the fog that swirls around them, a semi-transparent wall of spirit that forms a curtain against the world outside.

There is no longer a mountain. There is no longer sky.

There is only this seething mass of people, pushing in close, crushing together, the vibrant colors of jackets like the rainbow of a prayer flag against the darkness beyond.

In the heart of the throng, Sean pulls Carrie close, wrapping her in his long arms, his broad hands enveloping her and drawing her near. She comes to him without resistance. She buries her face in the hollow of his neck and feels her heart beating slowly and sluggishly against him, hears the damp echo of its reverberation in her ears.

His heartbeat does not respond in kind.

He is cool to the touch, and as they embrace she feels her own heat begin to dissipate and drain away, like snow melt trickling down a mountain path.

All around them, the others press close, their bodies beginning to sway, as if caught in some ancient rhythm, dancing to music that no one can hear.

They open their mouths in unison, heads thrown back to cry out into the night. Screams like howling wind and a low, deep moan that sounds like the shifting weight of mountains.

CHAPTER TWENTY-SEVEN

In the months that follow, Tom struggles with his memory.

Struggles in part because it is painful. But struggles, too, because he remembers things that are impossible, or that surely could not have happened as he recalls. The events are jumbled, and each time he recalls the story, each time he accesses those memories, they shift and change and reshape themselves. As if every time he recounts the final days on Everest, the story rewrites itself into something more rational, and he has no way of remembering what parts are true and what parts are rationalizations he added after the fact. And he has told the story so many times now.

To officials at the Embassy. To Carrie's family left behind in the States. To mountain guides and expedition members and paying clients, those people surprised and alarmed by his sudden decision to retire from mountaineering and those who have heard rumors about his final summit push and wonder whether they were true. He has told the story of Carrie and Sean Miller so many times now that he can recite it like a monologue, recalling the words of the last repetition more than the pure, agonizing memories of the actual event. And, on the balance, this feels right. It hurts less each time he tells the story, because each repetition draws him further and further from the truth.

The facts: On the night before a summit push, a storm descended on the mountain. Carrie woke in the night and left her tent, partially dressed and leaving her gear behind. Tom could not speculate as to why, but it was possible that she was sleep-walking or experiencing an episode of altitude psychosis. In any case, he had not heard her over the sound of his oxygen mask and the storm outside, and he did not realize that she was gone until morning. By the time they found her, she had succumbed to the elements. Her body was found with another unidentified climber, presumably lost to the same storm just below the peak.

That was the official version. Sanitized. Easily understood, for all that it left out.

A formal investigation into Carrie's death was conducted, but it was cursory at best. Officials investigate deaths on Everest, certainly, but they do not look at them too deeply. Mountaineering is a dangerous sport. There are waivers involved. No one is shocked to learn that a green climber, with little practical experience, would die in a storm on the world's tallest mountain. If anything, people are more shocked that she managed to make it as far as she did before succumbing to the weather. The place her body was found, in a snowy hollow just beneath the Hillary Step, was just over forty feet from the summit. She had come so close to reaching the top of the world, and that's the tragedy those who didn't know her tend to focus on when Tom retells this story. He lets them think what they want, because correcting them is not worth the effort or the pain.

It has been nearly a year since that doomed quest on Everest. Nearly two years since Tom stood in his apartment and tried to convince Sean that the mountain wasn't worth the effort.

He stands in that same apartment now, mountaineering gear scattered across his bed, spilling over onto the floor. Packs and jackets and boots, crampons and ice axes and bottles of oxygen.

He pulls his phone from his pocket, scrolling through his contacts. Waits for the line to connect. Even the ringing sounds distant, as if muffled by the miles between them.

What he has not told anyone about the events on the mountain, the part that he knows cannot be true but which he cannot force himself not to believe: he recognized the body of the second climber, too.

The gangling limbs, the auburn hair, the freckles cross-ing the pale skin like spatters of paint. Sean, impossibly, in-explicably, found in a drift of snow just a few hundred feet from Camp IV, a place a hundred people must have walked past since his death. Sean, his body resurfaced, materialized where it could not have been. But that wasn't the problem, isn't the reason Tom's hand is now shaking as he recalls it in his mind.

"Hey. It's Tom Fisher. Yeah. It's been a while, I know. But I'm ready now. I've booked the ticket and can get on a plane tomorrow?"

They exchange a few pleasantries, but his mind has wan-dered. As his gaze travels the gear assembled on his bed, his thoughts have turned back to Everest, to the pair of bodies lying tangled at the root of the Hillary Step. Carrie, with her arms wrapped around Sean, her face nuzzled into his chest. Sean with his arms around her shoulders, his chin atop her head. The pair of them embraced like the lovers of Pompeii, an eternity in one another's arms. Both of them frozen solid, pale and bloodless and caught in the ice, prepared to be sub-sumed by the mountain itself.

As though they had died together, sinking as one into the freshly fallen snow.

Tom had knelt in the snow beside them and wept. It was two days since Carrie's disappearance, two days spent in bitter anguish wondering after her fate, waiting for the weather to clear so he could get the answer he already knew. She had said she wanted to look there, and so he went to check, never suspecting she could have made it that distance on her own, and certainly not expecting to find her caught in the embrace of a man who had been dead for a year. The shock and the grief and the thin atmosphere convinced him that he was seeing things, and in the months that followed it became easier to believe that was true. It was easier to believe that the bodies could not have been entwined. That Carrie had merely found Sean, somehow—unlikely, but not impossible—and fallen beside him. It was the rational explanation, the logical one, and he might have believed it, if not for what he found tucked into Sean's parka, poking so invitingly from the pocket that it seemed almost begging Tom to find it and read it.

They were pages taken from the journal, crumpled and torn but still legible. The missing pages, the ones Carrie had accused Tom himself of removing though they had been torn out long before he or anyone else had gotten hold of the thing. Tom had taken them from Sean's body, had read the words and then, without knowing quite why, smoothed the paper down and carefully refolded it and tucked it into his pocket, assured that he would never share it with anyone. And he hasn't, not one word, though he can't bring himself to throw the paper out, either. Finds himself turning back to it, sneaking a peek in dark hours as a reminder that it was real.

He needs to know for certain. Needs to confirm what he saw on the mountain. Needs to make sense of it all.

He drags his attention back to the conversation at hand, remembers the weight and heat of the phone pressed to his ear. Feels himself smiling.

"Great. I know. Just one last time, you know? See you soon, Maya."

Undated - Pages Torn from Sean's Journal

If you are reading this, then I have been found.

I do not know who you are. There is no way for me to guarantee that this message will reach the hands of those I intended it for. A suicide note is an imprecise thing, and death leaves more to chance than I am comfortably accustomed to. I have never been one to relinquish control. But maybe that's how I ended up like this.

It was not my intention to die when I arrived in Nepal. I came to this mountain with every intention of climbing it, reaching its summit and feeling that rush of success at its conquest. I came here because climbing mountains is what I have always done, the thing that brings passion and meaning to my life, and Everest is the greatest and most infamous of mountains, even if it is not the most respectable among certain circles.

The point is, I did not come here to die.

But it has become increasingly clear that I will not be leaving this mountain. In the weeks I have camped here, making my arduous way up the slope, I have felt the hot breath of the creature at my back. I have seen the specters of the ghosts among the stones. These things are not hallucinations or exaggerations, hyperbole written to flesh out the pages of this journal. I am telling you this because, if you have found me, then perhaps you already know: they are real. You are not going insane.

Or maybe you are. Maybe I am. It is possible, I admit, that even the words written on this page mean nothing, empty ciphers scrawled in the handwriting of a man who has lost his mind.

But if you are reading this, it should not matter. If you are reading this, then I am dead, and the speculation over my final fate and the state of my mind up to that point is a burden on you to decipher, not for me to puzzle over. I hand this concern to you so that I may be freed of it, for I have other and more important matters to discuss.

Namely, when I realized that I would not come back from the peak of this mountain—when that certainty settled down over me, as warm and smothering as a blanket against the cold of night—I did not feel afraid. I felt a sense of deep and wonderful relief. And I realized, in feeling that, what a miserable shambles my life has become without my awareness.

I know about Carrie and Tom, of course.

You cannot love two people the way that I love them without knowing when something has happened, when something has changed between them and between you. Relationship dynamics are a gentle but lively force, a ghost that settles invisibly in the empty spaces between people but puts off its own heat and energy and light. When two people you love fall in love with each other, you can feel it, with the same deep certainty as you can feel the approach of your own death when faced with its inevitability.

So, Carrie. Tom. If you are reading this—if my wildest hope and dream is true, and if you indeed are the first people to find my body—then I will reiterate: I know. I have known from the beginning. Longer, maybe, than the two of you knew.

I would like to say here that I am not angry. I would like to say that I understand and that I forgive you both. I would like to say that it doesn't mean anything, and that we can talk it through and everything will be all right.

But I cannot say that, because it would be a lie, and the last words written in a dying man's journal should be the truth.

I cannot say that I forgive you, because I am cold and hungry and desperately uncomfortable. I am in the loneliest place on earth, and I cannot comfort myself with knowing that I will return home to a loving wife because I do not know whether she will even be there when I get back.

So. No. I do not forgive you.

You asked me once, Tom, why I would not wait for you. Why I chose to hire a Nepalese guide and summit the mountain without you when you would have been more than happy to take me the next season. Well, now you know. I hope you don't need me to spell this out.

I did not trust that I could ascend a mountain with you without giving in to the urge to shove you over the side of a cliff. I did not trust that I could reach a summit without leaving you for dead.

That is the truth, because I am a dying man, and the truth is important. It is all that I have left.

It is possible that my instincts are wrong, that I will not die here, that I will need to have this conversation with you face to face. And if that happens, then I will destroy these pages and fly home and talk with you both and maybe we can even work this out.

But I don't think that will happen.

I think that I will die on this mountain. And when I do, I think that you will come for me—you and Carrie both, maybe, because she was never good at letting things go, not when they belonged to her.

I think that you will come for me, and find my body somewhere in the snow, and when you do I hope you find these pages and read them and understand.

I hope the mountain reaches up into you and holds you in place, too.

It won't let me leave. I hope it won't let you leave, either.

ACKNOWLEDGEMENTS

This book grew out of a combination of fascination and obsession, and it would not exist without the writing of Jon Krakauer and Nick Heil, and the numerous Sherpa interviews, YouTube videos, documentaries, and articles I pored over in my attempts to understand what drives men to conquer mountains. Any errors are my own.

I would like to thank my editor, Antonia Rachel Ward, for her keen eye and unwavering enthusiasm for this project. I'd also like to thank all of the beta readers who gave invaluable insights as this book came together, and the entirety of The Bleeding Pen writer's Discord, without whom I don't think I'd have weathered these last few years nearly so well.

T.L. Bodine, December 2022

ABOUT THE AUTHOR

T.L. Bodine is the author of RIVER OF SOULS and its sequel HOUSE OF LAZARUS, the Wattpad-exclusive THE HOUND, and many other tales of horror. She's interested in uncanny, fantastic things, and the way real people with real problems interact with them.

When not writing, she can usually be found watching horror movies, playing story-heavy video games, or experimenting in the kitchen.

She lives in New Mexico with her husband, David, and two small dogs.